Last Carol of the Season

Claremary P. Sweeney

Publisher's Information

EBookBakery Books

Author contact: claremarypsweeney@yahoo.com
Author blog: AroundZuzusBarn.com

Cover Design and Map by Zachary Perry - ZPerryDesigns.com

ISBN 978-1-938517-84-6
1. Mystery. 2. Murder. 3. Claremary P. Sweeney
4. South County Rhode Island 5. Wakefield, Rhode Island
6. Holiday Season

Last Carol of the Season

Claremary P. Sweeney

For Charley
who fills my world with Christmas Spirit all year long

and

*for all the people who are there for you when those who
should be are not.*

Main Street in the Village of Wakefield, Circa 1900

CHAPTER TITLES

Friday, November 24

1

Do You See What I See?

She stood a moment, eyes closed, breathing in the pungent lemony smell of polished wood before switching on the overhead lights. The staccato clack of her boot heels against the worn planked flooring followed her across the expanse of the main level into her office in the back corner of the 1891 Queen Anne styled building. She'd come in earlier than usual to get a head start on Black Friday - the official beginning of the holiday retail season.

Beatrice loved working in the historic building. As a child, she'd spent many Saturday mornings shopping here with her mother. Some of the smaller stores in the town had been forced to close during the past decade. Competition with big box stores was hurting the local mom and pop businesses. But Kenyon's was different. Established in 1868, the old-fashioned department store had become an institution that promised always to be there on the village's Main Street. After her own thirty-nine years of weathering life's uncertainties, Beatrice took solace in the thought that some things would never change.

She'd been promoted to assistant manager in October – entrusted with the keys to open and close the store. Living nearby on Kenyon Avenue at the crest of the hill behind the store, she could walk the short distance from her house to work every day.

Beatrice removed her gloves and hat and began searching the oak, roll-top desk to see where she'd placed the back door key to the office in her hurry to get home on Wednesday. It was nowhere to be found. She was acutely aware that her memory continued to worsen with each month's passing. She patted her coat pocket to make certain the front door key was there.

Beatrice turned up the thermostat to warm the building, then knelt to open the safe. Counting out the bills and coins, she prepared the tills for each cash register and carried one down the double staircase to the bargain basement, setting it on the counter. An eerie feeling washed over her and she tilted her head, listening attentively to floorboards creaking above her. The groans of the old furnace coupled with a sharp howling of the wind from outside interrupted her thoughts.

Returning to the office, she grabbed a second till and headed up the broad staircase to the women's department. Ping! The cash register sprang open and she deposited the money into the drawer. The air was frigid and she rubbed her hands together to warm them. She picked up a lone woolen glove from the floor. It had no tag. She tossed it into the wire bin with other items to be matched, priced and reshelved, then switched on the lights and started down the stairs. In her rush, Beatrice failed to notice the pale, lifeless hand jutting out from under the red and white gingham curtain of the lady's dressing room.

Phil's was packed. People stood at the door waiting for an empty booth or a seat at the counter. The waitress brought a carafe of coffee to the window table where Kara, Ruth and Sophia were discussing plans for Ruth's wedding to Sophia's brother-in-law, Rick Carnavale.

Detective Lieutenant Kara Langley was finding it surprisingly pleasant to be able to spend more time with friends. She'd recently taken a leave of absence from her job on the South Kingstown Police Department, although Captain Lewis had requested she be available for consultation.

Kara passed the carafe to Ruth Eddleman who poured herself a cup. Ruth, a professor of English at the University of Rhode Island, had first met Kara when she was a student at the school. Upon graduating from the university, Kara left for a job on the New York City Police Force. After a few years in the big city, she returned to the small village of Kingston and they renewed their friendship. Ruth had introduced Kara to Stewart. "A perfect match," she'd proudly proclaimed when they announced they would be tying the knot seven years ago this month.

On the first shopping day of the season, the three women were deep in conversation about Ruth's impending wedding, which Sophia Carnavale had enthusiastically volunteered to oversee. She had everything well in hand. Although the bride-to-be had suggested a small, intimate affair, Sophia's definition of "intimate" was apparently not the same as Ruth's. Everyone they knew from town and from the university's English and art departments was invited to a service on Christmas Night followed by a receiving line, champagne and hors d'oeuvres in the church hall after the ceremony. They were going over the list of those who would be attending.

"Sophia, has anyone sent regrets? It appears as though everyone on this list is coming." Ruth took a large gulp of coffee from her mug.

"The Whitakers are tentative. They're expecting their first grandchild and they may have to travel to Connecticut. But it's a first baby and Jasmine Whitaker has never been on time for anything in her life so, yes, it looks like everyone will be there." The official wedding organizer grinned brightly across the table at her two friends.

"You've done a marvelous job, Sophia. It's only been three months since Rick and Ruth got engaged. I think you'd make an awesome wedding planner. You've missed your true calling," Kara praised her friend.

"Don't encourage her," Ruth said. "They need you at the hospital, Sophia. I don't think the place could function properly without you. The population of South County would plummet."

She nodded emphatically in agreement, and Kara and Ruth shared a quick glance. They'd long accepted the fact that humility was not Sophia's strong suit.

"Gino is touching base with the caterers tomorrow." She removed a laminated sheet of paper from her loose-leaf binder to give to Ruth. "Check over the food on that list and tell me if you want him to order anything else."

"I think this will do fine." Ruth scanned the pages. "Looks like we'll be feeding a small army."

"Don't worry about the cost. I told you, it's our gift to you. Gino has lots of connections on The Hill and tons of people owe him favors."

"I'll write you a check for the champagne, before I forget." Kara opened her bag.

"Don't bother - all taken care of. Gino knows a guy who knows a guy who knows a guy."

Providence's Federal Hill had long been known as the home of La Cosa Nostra, although its reputation had waned in the decades since the head Don, Raymond Loreda Salvatore Patriarca, Sr. had gone to his just reward in 1984.

It was Kara's turn to gulp down a mouthful of juice and whisper to Ruth, "I'm not even going to ask."

"The flowers and cake are ordered. Rick has the rings. Stewart's picking up the tuxes. Your dress is altered and ready. I need to hem and do a final fitting for Kara's. Now, all we have to do is sit back and enjoy the holidays." Sophia closed the binder as the waitress delivered breakfast.

"Do you have much shopping to get done?" Ruth asked both women.

"I'd like to pick up some gifts from Dove and Distaff. They have a new line of alpaca goods and the gloves and socks are luxurious. I've already bought a dark green sweater for Gino and a matching one in navy blue for Rick, since they're twins." Sophia crunched up a slice of bacon to mix into her scrambled egg before taking a bite.

"Matching sweaters? How adorable! Won't Rick just love that?" Kara chuckled.

"It will bring back fond memories for both of them. I found a whole album of photos from their childhood and in almost every one, their mother dressed them alike," Sophia informed her.

"I would pay to be in the room with Rick when you bring that album out, Sophia," Kara declared, taking out her wallet.

Under the table, Ruth kicked her friend. "Ouch!" Kara leaned down to rub her ankle. "Sometimes it's hard to remember they're twins. They don't look alike and they really don't sound alike."

"They're fraternal twins and Gino hung around the corners with a tough crowd when they were growing up in New York. Rick spent most of his younger days volunteering at any museum that would take him in," Sophia said.

Ruth added, "But what they both have in common is a love of art and they're each talented in that area. Just in different ways."

Sophia agreed with her friend. "I've been thinking of making a slide show of Ruth and Rick through the years ending with them getting together. We could watch it at the reception."

"Sophia, I'm sorry to say I don't have many photos of me in my younger years," Ruth said.

"That's okay. If you give me what you have, I can get pictures on the Internet of babies and kids doing strange things. I'll just super-impose your head on their bodies."

"Now, that would be entertaining!" Kara deftly moved her leg to avoid another warning kick from the future bride.

Ruth sighed and decided to turn the conversation back to the present. "I saw a hand-made pewter brooch in the shape of a snowflake at Kenyon's. Something my mother would like. There are red holly berries around the edges."

"Sounds lovely. We can pick it up after we finish breakfast - before the crowds descend on the stores. Stewart and I aren't exchanging gifts this year. We're surprising each other with tickets to something. There are a few shows at the Contemporary Theatre I'm sure he'd enjoy," Kara said.

Ruth applauded. "I like that idea – time spent together. What better present could you get?"

"Diamonds - or better yet, sapphires surrounded by diamonds." Sophia extended her left hand for them to admire her rings. "You and Stewart have been spending a lot of time together lately since you've been on leave from the police force. You should be sick of each other by now." Sophia nibbled on a piece of toast. She raised an eyebrow and asked pointedly, "When are you planning on going back to work?"

"I don't know if I am," Kara answered avoiding her friend's stare.

"Well then, it's fortunate for the townsfolk that nothing serious has happened in the past three months," Sophia said.

"Detective Sullivan's been handling things quite well without me." Kara took a packet of raspberry jam from the metal holder and began slowly peeling off the plastic top.

"I'd think you'd be bored with no crimes to solve," Sophia continued needling her friend.

"Professor Hill's been letting me work with him at the forensics lab on campus. And I plan to audit the Modern American Novel Course Ruth and Arthur are co-teaching next semester. I've been reading the books on the syllabus."

Arthur was a Pulitzer Prize winning author who had come to live a quiet life in Kingston away from the rapid pace of New York City. Ruth had been trying to convince him to teach a class with her for years and he had finally agreed.

Sophia wasn't impressed. "You never struck me as the stay-at-home type." She watched as Kara fiddled with the packet. "Are you going to put that goo on your toast or just sit playing with your food?"

Kara tossed it across the table at her and Sophia cooly responded by catching it, taking Kara's uneaten slice of toast from her plate, and slathering it with red jam.

Ruth quickly changed the subject. "Rick and I are looking forward to spending the winter break up in the Berkshires. I think we'll get in some skiing and snowmobiling. I'm sure Rick will want to do some photography and I can work on my poetry manuscript."

"Gino and I would be glad to get out our snowmobile and join you but I'm pretty sure the hospital will be busy. Flu season's already started. I'd never get the time off," Sophia informed them.

"Thank goodness for small mercies," Kara leaned in to whisper in Ruth's ear as she took the last slice of toast from her plate and offered it to Sophia with a smile.

They paid for breakfast and headed for the department store a short distance away. Sophia grabbed an orange crosswalk flag and played crossing guard for Ruth and Kara, mischievously poking at them to make sure they stayed between the lines in the street leading to the front door of Kenyon's.

Along with a middle-aged couple and two teen-aged girls, they were the first customers of the day. Ruth went immediately to the jewelry counter and pointed out the brooch, then waited for the saleswoman to wrap her gift. Kara was browsing the knitwear in the baby department when Sophia call out, "Kara! Come quick!"

Kara bounded up the staircase to the second floor where her friend was frozen in place in front of the lady's dressing room. A body lay on the floor. A young male clerk and the two teens stood gawking from the other side of the room.

Kara knelt by the body. She rose slowly, took Sophia's arm and calmly directed them all to follow her down the stairs. She phoned the police station on her cell and gave instructions to Leo, the dispatcher.

Everyone gathered together in the accessories department on the first floor. Kara asked that they remain there until the police arrived to speak with them. The manager emerged from her office and Kara pulled her aside, explaining the situation. Kara recognized her — Beatrice Pruitt. A few years back, she'd been sent to the woman's house on a domestic violence call. She'd heard that Pruitt had undergone counseling at the family resource center in town and had eventually filed for a divorce from her husband. Kara noticed dark purple marks not well hidden by the black turtle-neck sweater and she wondered if the woman had gotten back with her ex or was now involved in another bad relationship.

"There's a body upstairs in one of the dressing rooms. I've called the police. They'll want to talk with your staff and the customers in the store. Could you send someone to lock the front and side doors and wait at the back of the building to let the officers in?"

"A body in the dressing room? Has there been an accident? Why wasn't I notified?"

"It's been there a while."

"But I've been in the store since before eight this morning. I opened up around 7:45. No one else was here. How could this have happened?"

"The police will be questioning the people who are in the store. They'll need to use your office to do the initial interviews."

"Of course." She hesitated nervously and then asked one of the clerks to come with her to lock the doors.

Kara quickly scanned the first floor. Kara told Ruth to send the officers upstairs when they arrived and she returned to stand guard over the body in the dressing room.

Outside, sirens blared as she began slowly turning in place, checking everything carefully. Walking toward the body, she surveyed the immediate area. One of the panels in the dressing room's three-way-mirror was cracked. The body lay slumped on the floor, the torso leaning outward, its left hand extended slightly into the room.

Detective Sullivan and Sergeant Shwinnard were the first to arrive. Ruth filled them in on the situation before they went upstairs, leaving the rest of the team to take care of the witnesses.

"Detective Langley, nice to see you, although the circumstances leave something to be desired."

Kara shook her old partners' hands. "I was just doing some early Christmas shopping. It's really good to see both of you." She stepped back, turning to leave and let them do their jobs.

"Lieutenant, could you stay here until the medical examiner arrives? I'm sure you could fill us in on anything you may have observed," Sullivan said as he took out his notebook.

"The manager told me she opened the store around 7:45AM and didn't notice anything amiss. I'm sure you'll get more details from her statement. I was on the main floor when I heard my friend call out. I ran upstairs to find Sophia Carnavale outside the dressing room looking down on the body. She'll tell you what she observed when you question her."

Kara once again started to leave and then added, "About the manager, Beatrice Pruitt - tell Harry to check the bruises on her neck - ask her where they came from. And the victim, his name is Sherman Pruitt, I recognized him. He's Beatrice's ex-husband. He and I have some past history. A domestic violence call. The last time I saw him, he was on a stretcher being transported to the hospital to be treated for a broken jaw."

"Did the wife fight back?"

"No, the jaw was my doing."

After initial statements had been taken, the customers and sales clerks were allowed to leave. The store would be closed for the remainder of the day. Kara sat in the office with Beatrice, waiting for Harry Henderson, the state medical examiner, to finish upstairs. Detective Sullivan had sent Shwinnard to request that Lieutenant Langley remain with the manager. He wanted Kara with Mrs. Pruitt when they brought her upstairs to identify the victim. At the moment, Beatrice was still unaware it was her ex-husband's body in the dressing room.

Harry appeared and crooked his index finger. "Detective Langley, could we have a word?" A flash of recognition came over the manager's face on hearing the woman sitting with her addressed as "detective".

They moved discreetly away from the office. Henderson was the first to speak. "You're looking well, my dear. Professor Hill informs me you've been working with him unofficially on a case or two. I warned him that you could end up with his job."

"No danger of that. Like you, Harry, the professor is indispensable."

"Sullivan tells me you know the victim."

"Sherman Pruitt. He was married to Beatrice, the store's assistant manager. They've been divorced a few years. I'd heard he'd moved to Exeter. Got hired at Mercy Brown High School.

"So what's he doing in Wakefield at her place of work? Do you think there could be some connection?"

"I don't know."

"You noticed marks on her neck?"

"Before you bring her up to identify the body, I think now would be a good time to ask her about that." Kara hesitated, "Have you determined cause of death? I noticed the hair and blood in the cracked glass on the broken mirror."

"You're thinking it might have been an accident?" Harry raised his bushy eyebrows waiting to hear her response.

"He had to hit the mirror with some force, so there must have been some kind of altercation. Still, that doesn't rule out an accident."

"Mebbe," he muttered adding, "but that theory doesn't explain the metal spindle imbedded in his spinal cord."

"I guess it wouldn't," Kara agreed, hiding her surprise at the revelation as she followed him back to the office.

"Mrs. Pruitt, I'm Doctor Henderson, the state medical examiner." She stood to shake his hand. He remarked, "Appears you've got some bruising under your chin. Mind if I take a look?" He turned the collar down and observed the marks, which went all the way round to the back. "Somebody's had his hands around your neck, Mrs. Pruitt. Care to tell me what happened?"

Beatrice looked at Kara and acknowledged her. "I didn't recognize you, Detective. It was some time ago and you were in uniform." She explained to Henderson, "We know each other from when I was married. Sherm, my husband – ex-husband - sometimes hit me when he had too much to drink. He showed up at the house yesterday. I hadn't seen him in months. He was drunk and his girlfriend had tossed him out. He was looking for a handout. Some money and a place to have a Thanksgiving meal. When I told him to leave, he grabbed me by the throat. Like I said, he was drunk. My friend, Ed Tucker, threatened to call the police and he left."

"What time was that?"

"Early evening. It was already dark, so, maybe around six o'clock."

"Was that the last you saw of him, Mrs. Pruitt?"

"He didn't return."

"Mrs. Pruitt, I'd like you to come with Detective Langley and me."

She looked questioningly at Kara but followed them up the stairs to where the medics had placed the body on a stretcher. He waited until she was next to him and then uncovered the face. For a few moments, she remained rigid, her eyes unblinking and then spoke in a cold, hard voice, "That's Sherman. Sherman Pruitt. My ex-husband."

At the police station, Kara recorded her official statement and went to stand outside the interrogation room with Sergeant Shwinnard watching through the glass as Detective Sullivan questioned Beatrice Pruitt.

"Could you tell me about your last encounter with Sherman Pruitt?"

"I had just finished preparing the Thanksgiving meal for my friend, Ed Tucker, and his family. He has two young children, Jeff and Cindy. They were all at the house. His wife left him last year, just around the holidays. We've been friends since elementary school. He's not a great cook and I asked them to come by for dinner. The kids were helping to bring the food to the table and there was a knock on the front door. I went to answer it and Sherman was standing outside on the porch. I could smell the liquor on his breath and he was acting like we were best buddies. He pushed past me into the living room and told me Vida, his girlfriend, had thrown him out again and he knew I'd be alone, so maybe we could have dinner together. I informed him I had guests and asked him to leave. He became angry and told me I could certainly make room for one more. I said 'No' and that's when he grabbed me by the throat and began hollering. Ed came from the kitchen and when Sherman saw him, he let go of me and ran out the door swearing and cussing on the front lawn and then he got into his car and took off."

"What time was this, Mrs. Pruitt?"

"I would say about 6PM."

"And you didn't see him at any time after that?"

"No, we had our dinner and Cindy and Jeff watched a movie. Ed and I talked 'til around eight when he took the kids home. We both had work the next day."

"You were alone for the rest of the night."

"Yes."

"Did you leave your house at any time?"

After a slight hesitation, she brushed strands of greying hair from her eyes and shook her head. "No".

"Did anyone stop by or phone?"

"No."

"Do you have any idea how Mr. Pruitt could have gained access to the store?"

"I remember thinking the building was colder than it usually is when I open up. Maybe he got in through a window?"

"Did you find any windows unlocked or broken when you were getting the store ready for customers?" Sullivan leaned forward in his chair.

"I wasn't paying close attention. I turned up the thermostat and switched on the lights. I mostly concentrated on placing the money into the tills for the cashiers. We still use the old-fashioned cash registers. They're original - antique. Although, we do have charge card machines on the counters. You can't run a successful business without taking charge cards, nowadays."

"Except for the cold, you didn't notice anything unusual?"

"When I was in the basement, I thought I heard footsteps coming from the first floor. I'd left the front door unlocked. I got an eerie feeling. Like something bad was going to happen. Sometimes, I have premonitions. I'm usually right. Something terrible always happens." She shook her head in disbelief.

Kara considered this for a moment and concluded the woman could be right. Bad things did seem to follow in her wake.

Beatrice Pruitt was released after signing her statement and being fingerprinted. Kara waited in her old office. Although Carl Sullivan was using it in her absence, nothing really had changed since she'd left in August. He was neater than she'd been and the paperwork was organized in three compact stacks on the desk. She knew his methods: one pile for Do It Now! A second one for Do It Later. And a third for There's Always Tomorrow. Unfortunately, for some people, tomorrow never comes. This unfortunately had rung true during her last case when a young woman died. What should have been done now had been put off to later, the result proving fatal.

Kara took full responsibility and had decided to use some of her accumulated time off to reassess her own life choices. Except for her honeymoon, she'd not taken a vacation or sick day during her years on the force. Carl called her every day to apprise her of any ongoing cases. He fully expected her to return soon. She was not sure if that would ever happen.

The door opened and Sullivan and Shwinnard entered. She took the seat next to Shwinnard. Carl sat behind the desk in her old chair.

"So, what did you make of her statement?"

Kara let Shwinnard go first. "We'll only be able to confirm what she said after we speak with Ed Tucker. Detective Brown is with him now. No matter what Tucker says, she has no one to alibi her later that night. And she certainly had motive and opportunity. It doesn't look good for her. I was surprised by her behavior when she identified the body. I got the feeling she really hated the guy." He turned toward Kara.

"She has good reason to despise him. He abused her. She had a breakdown. She lost custody of her son because of him."

"I agree," Sullivan added. "We still need the forensic reports and we're lining up interviews with neighbors and people who knew him from work. I'm planning on visiting with Vida Koranski, the girlfriend. But right now, Mrs. Pruitt certainly is a person of interest."

Kara stood up. Shwinnard helped her on with her coat. Sullivan came from around the desk to shake her hand.

"You two are a great team. I have a gift certificate to the Mews Tavern. Maybe we can meet up like we used to for burgers and beer next week?"

"Sounds good. I'll phone you tonight when I get home," Sullivan called after her as she left the room.

The boy hoisted the Christmas box down from the closet shelf in the hall and opened the flaps. He began to unpack the lights, bringing them, one at a time, to the windows in the apartment. He plugged them in. A bulb was missing from one of the candles.

His aunt called to him, "Come in here and take a break, Buddy. I poured you a mug of cocoa."

In the large kitchen, Suzanne Tetreault was slipping another aluminum sheet filled with sugar cookie angels into the oven. "There's a plate of star shaped ones that needs decorating. I don't think you'll mind tasting a few before we add the sprinkles."

The doorbell rang. "I'll get that. The marshmallows are over there." She pointed to a large, silver tin on the counter.

He sat at the table and added a handful of mini marshmallows into his mug, watching them float around and melt into the dark chocolate. He took a sip and licked the sticky white mustache from his upper lip.

She looked to see that the boy had not followed, then stepped into the hall closing the door behind her. Beatrice pushed a crumpled up scarf and glove to one side and lowered herself wearily onto the bench.

Suzanne sat down next to her. "I knew you'd get in touch. We saw the commotion at the store on our way out this morning. What happened?"

"I've been at the police station."

"Police?"

"They just dropped me off at home. I needed to take a walk."

"Do you want to come in?"

"No, I've got to get back. I have to call Ed to see if he can come over and help me get my car started. The battery was dead this morning when I went out to get some packages I'd left in the car yesterday. I might have forgotten to shut the door. I've done that before. The light probably drained the battery and … "

"Bea, you're rambling. Why were you at the police station?"

"There was a body in one of the dressing rooms when I got to work this morning."

"A body? How awful! Are you okay? That must have been a shock for you."

"I didn't know. I opened up the store and I didn't know he was there. And then a customer found him and the police came."

"Was it an accident?"

"I don't know. They didn't tell me anything. He was just lying there. And there was blood on the mirror. He must have bumped his head. They brought me upstairs to identify him."

"You identified him for the police? You knew him?"

"It was Sherman."

"Sherman? What was he doing in the store?"

"I don't know, Sue. They asked me questions and let me go. I think he may have been murdered."

"Bea, if that's what they're thinking, you need to get a lawyer."

"I know. Ed's got a friend who works for a firm in Providence. He's going to get me the information. Could you do me a favor? Could you call Evelyn? She's living in Maine. Here's her number."

"That's okay, I already have her number in my contacts. Did you give it to the police?"

"No, I said I didn't know how to get in touch with anyone in his family. I wanted you to call her first and break the news before the cops get the info from Vida. Evelyn hasn't seen her dad in years, but someone needs to tell her he's dead. And I was hoping you'd do that for me. She always liked you. You were so good to her when she lived with me."

"Of course I'll call her. Is there anything else I can do for you, Bea?"

"No, I'll keep in touch and tell you what's happening." She stood up stiffly and hesitated a moment. "How's Buddy?"

"Good. He's doing really well. Still at the top of his class and he loves being in the band." Suzanne waited but when Beatrice made no comment she added, "We've been decorating for Christmas."

"I saw the candles lit in the windows. Such a nice tradition. The Irish brought it here with them, you know. Candles to guide Mary and Joseph into their home – to let people know they're welcome inside."

Suzanne zippered her sister-in-law's jacket and tucked in the scarf around her neck. "November's been terribly cold. Try to stay warm, Bea."

Back inside the apartment, Suzanne called out, "The tree looks beautiful, Buddy. I'm glad we decided not to get that artificial one on sale at Home Depot last January. There's nothing like the smell of a real pine tree. I'll just be another minute, I have to make a quick phone call." She went into her bedroom and closed the door.

He brought his cocoa into the living room. Pushing aside the lace curtain, he stood watching as his mother crossed the street and disappeared up Kenyon Avenue leaving her footprints in the soft snow that had begun to cover the ground.

Saturday, November 25

2

MAKING A LIST, CHECKING IT TWICE

Kara hadn't slept well, waking at 5AM as she'd done every morning when she was working. She'd been going over in her mind all that had happened from the time they'd walked into Kenyon's the previous day. She sat in the den looking over her note cards. Store had been cold but no windows were open. Lights were on. Two teenage girls at top of stairs. Young salesman close by - Was he helping the girls? Watching them? Chatting with them? Why had he not noticed anything? Sophia standing just outside the dressing room - curtain open - body propped against mirror. Mirror cracked - blood and hair - not much blood. Victim - not wearing a coat - where was his coat?

She closed her eyes to see if she remembered anything out of place. Anything on the floor? Any clothes fallen off the circular racks placed around the room? Wire basket by the counter, clothes inside – pink sweater, paisley scarf, orange glove, black polka-dotted bow tie, red and green striped Christmas socks. The counter - cash register, charge card machine on left side - no receipts, no sales tickets. Why was he there?

She took the other pile of index cards and began to sort through them. Beatrice Pruitt, manager – NO ALIBI. Opened up early at 7:45AM - Didn't notice anything out of place. Went floor to floor setting up cash registers. Turned on heat, lights. In office – didn't hear Sophia call out. Didn't realize her ex-husband was in store dead. Reaction when identifying body - Surprise? Hate? Marks on neck from ex choking her previous day.

She had other piles of cards but two words on the one she picked up were in bold, capital letters: NO ALIBI! Had means, motive, opportunity.

Motive? Kara wondered if Beatrice had ever been given back custody of her son. She thought about getting dressed and going to the station to talk with Carl.

"Hey! You're up early." Stewart stood in his robe and yawned. "What've you been doing?"

"Making a list," she said.

"Great idea! I thought we might send out e-cards this year. It's greener - more environmentally responsible." He kissed her on the forehead.

"Sounds like a plan," she said, not correcting his assumption she was working on their Christmas card list.

"I'll brew us some tea. And what about I pop some cinnamon buns in the oven? Looks like a perfect day to do some shopping and maybe cut down our tree. What do you think?"

"I think you're full of great ideas this morning. I'm all yours for the whole day." She swept the cards into the desk and closed the drawer.

Detective Sullivan looked over the list of names and addresses of people still needing to be interviewed. The previous day, the team had covered most of the surrounding neighborhood. Except for Healy's Newspaper and Magazine Store around the corner on Robinson Avenue, none of the small businesses had been open on Thanksgiving.

"The manager at Healy's closed a little after ten," Detective Brown said. "I showed him the photos. He mentioned he didn't have many customers and would have remembered Pruitt if he'd been in the store. And he didn't recognize Pruitt's car."

"Did anyone speak with Ms. Tetreault, the woman who lives in apartment 211 across from Kenyon's? I don't see a statement from her," Sullivan asked Shwinnard.

"I visited the apartments in the Bell Block Building. She was the only one who wasn't at home. I was going to stop by today," the sergeant said.

"That's okay, I can go by this morning on my way to Exeter to speak with Vida Koransky. Sergeant Carlyle interviewed her yesterday and tells me the woman is quite a character. Who is in charge of contacting the teachers at the school where Sherman Pruitt worked?" Sullivan asked.

"I got the directory with their names and numbers and I'm going to speak with some of the faculty today," Shwinnard told him.

The phone rang and Harry Henderson was on the other end. He cut to the quick. "Our victim died of a stab wound to his spinal cord. Marks on his chest indicate he was shoved hard and probably fell against the mirror. But the bump on his head was superficial. It wouldn't have killed him. No sign of broken bones except for the old jaw injury." He cleared his throat and continued, "He died around 10PM on Thursday. Stomach contents show he ate a Thanksgiving meal of cheeseburgers, onion rings and french fries."

"That would match up with the wrappers we found in his car. What about liquor?"

"There was some absorbed into his system. I'll get back to you on that later. I thought you'd want the preliminary report."

"Thanks, Harry. Any info helps right now. Especially knowing time of death. That rules out his coming in the front door in the morning while his ex was in the store's basement."

"Is Detective Langley around, today?"

"No, I was supposed to call her last night, but I was swamped. I'll contact her today. I'd like to know her thoughts on Beatrice Pruitt."

"I suppose that could be complicated, asking for her input - since Kara's a witness," Henderson said.

"That and the fact she once broke the guy's jaw certainly could be seen as a conflict of interest. But I'd still like any help she can give us. You know, it's not the same around here without her."

"When you speak with her, tell her I said, 'Hi'".

Sullivan made three more calls. Kara didn't answer and he left a brief voice message. Vida Koranski wasn't at all happy to hear his voice. Suzanne Tetreault was home but informed him she would be going out in the afternoon. He said he'd be there in fifteen minutes.

"Buddy, I made a grocery list. Would you go to Belmont's Market and get me a few things? I'm afraid I might run out of brown sugar and I'll need more vanilla. I can't go myself. I've got to keep baking. I still have five more batches to put in the oven for the cookie swap this afternoon."

"I've got to stop by the Baptist church to see when they'll need help setting up the outdoor crèche for next weekend. Shouldn't take me long. I'll do the shopping right after I'm done there."

"Then, could you go up to Mooresfield Road and pick up two packages of the Georgia pecans at Fayerweather House? We'll need them to make our fruitcake cookies tomorrow." She handed him another twenty-dollar bill. He took the money and the list and gave his aunt a kiss on the cheek. "It's fruitcake weather!" He called out grabbing another gingerbread cookie before leaving.

Sullivan stood on the sidewalk looking up at the architectural features of the 1899 Bell Block Building. Until 1890, it had been the George Babcock Boarding House and Livery Stable. His great grandmother remembered a time when the third floor had been a dance hall and vaudeville theatre and she told him stories of meeting her friends to go rollerskating there on Saturday afternoons. His daydreaming was interrupted when a boy on a bicycle came from the driveway separating the Bell Block from Sheldon's Furniture Store. The teenager narrowly avoided running him down.

"Sorry, man."

"My fault. I wasn't watching where I was going." He let the boy pass by.

Sullivan walked over to the window of Sheldon's where, as a child, he'd gone with his mom and his dad to shop for the furniture they still had in their living room. He vividly remembered sitting on a rocking chair in the store window as a salesman reminisced about the past.

"Son, you ever seen them move a building?" the old man asked.

Carl had to admit it was something he'd never experienced in all his eight years.

"Well, in 1899, using only oxen and manpower, Thomas Sweeney brought this structure from west of the Saugatucket Bridge down Main Street. The move took men and oxen three entire weeks. Amazingly, nothing inside the store was broken in the process. Villagers were even allowed to climb ladders up into the salesrooms to do their shopping. They drove their wagons underneath the jacked up building until it was safely wedged between Bell Block and S.G. Wright Apothecary. The owners held a grand reopening at Christmastime in 1899."

The salesman went to his office and brought back a photo album with pictures from that time. Sullivan smiled at the memories of that day when he sat rocking in the window of the store listening to the old-timer's tales of Main Street.

Candles were now lit in the large windows above the storefronts. From where he stood, if he turned, he could see the old Louis Bell House on a rise just behind the department store. Sullivan was surrounded by history. He'd grown up in the neighborhood and he and his wife were raising their two boys in a home next door to his parents on a side street off Kenyon Avenue. He liked the familiarity of it all and wanted his boys to have the same type of childhood he'd enjoyed. He rang the outside buzzer to be let into the building.

The smell of gingerbread filled the stairway to Suzanne Tetreault's apartment. His knock was answered immediately as though she'd been lying in wait for him on the other side of the door. He offered his identification but she'd already moved aside for him to come into the living room. Bing Crosby was crooning, "Santa Claus is Coming to Town" in harmony with the Andrews Sisters. A seven-foot, decorated evergreen was in a corner of the room, its bubble lights flickering, a glittering silver and blue mercury star perched on the top. She greeted him as though they'd known each other forever.

"Come in. Let me take your coat. Let's go into the kitchen. I've been baking since yesterday. I'm getting ready for the big cookie swap at church this afternoon. Do you want tea, coffee or hot chocolate? Or a cold glass of milk?" Trays and boxes of cookies covered every available surface in the cozy kitchen.

She was one of those women who took a deep breath before talking, seldom pausing in the conversation to let the listener get a word in. His grandmother was much like that only she spoke in Italian and broken English. His Nonni spent most of December in the kitchen baking, her grandchildren sitting around the table kneading, rolling, cutting, decorating.

"Milk, please." He sat and let her go on talking until she finally settled into the chair across the table from him and stopped to take a sip of tea.

"Mrs. Tetreault ..."

"Miss Tetreault. I never married. I was engaged once but ..."

He jumped in, "Miss Tetreault, as I explained on the phone, we're speaking to people in the neighborhood and asking if they'd observed anything Thursday night or during the early morning hours of Friday? There was a break-in across the street."

"At Kenyon's. I'd heard about that. We weren't here most of Friday. We had errands and shopping to get done. And we went to bed early when we returned home on Thursday night."

"We?"

"Yes, my nephew, Buddy lives with me. My brother's boy. He's lived here since he was really little. He's a teenager now. A good boy. He can't do enough to help me. I don't know what I'd do without him."

"His parents are dead?"

"His father, my brother, Daniel, died when Buddy was an infant. His mother had a breakdown. She couldn't take care of herself, let alone a baby. We decided it was best for him to be with me. Take some more cookies. Do you have children, Detective?"

"I have two boys. Connor and Billy."

"I'll just put some of these cookies in a bag so you can bring them home with you." She bustled around while they talked.

"Thank you. So, you didn't notice anyone hanging around outside the store Thursday night or Friday morning?"

"We weren't here, Detective. We went to Pawtucket for Thanksgiving dinner with family and got home late. The bedrooms are on the other side, away from the street, so we wouldn't have seen or heard anything after we went to sleep. What time was the break-in, may I ask?"

"We're not sure right now. That's why we're interviewing people to find out if anyone remembers seeing something suspicious that night."

"We were in bed around ten and there was no one on the street when we got home, Detective."

"So you have family in Pawtucket? My wife, Jess grew up there."

"My family still lives on Calder Street - Saint Cecilia's Parish. The Tetreaults are a big family - Canadian French from Quebec. We always spend Thanksgiving together – eating and playing cards."

"Thanks, Miss Tetreault. Here's my number. Please call if you or your nephew remember anything that could help us."

She placed the card in the pocket of her apron just under the embroidered Rudolph. She walked him to the front door and handed him the bag.

"Buddy and I are making fruitcake cookies tomorrow. I'll make sure we put some aside for you."

In the car, Sullivan phoned the station and spoke with the dispatcher. "Leo, could you have whoever's in the office get an address and telephone number for me? Tetreault on Calder Street in Pawtucket. Thanks. Just put the information on my desk." When he hung up, he called Kara.

"Hey, I hope I'm not bothering you."

"We're roaming around Highland Farms looking for the perfect Christmas tree."

"I just have one question for you. Do you remember the name of Beatrice Pruitt's son? The one you mentioned seeing when you made the call to their house?"

"Buddy. Buddy Tetreault."

"Thanks, Kara." He decided to make a change of plans. The next visit on his list would be to Bea Pruitt.

When Sullivan arrived at the house, Ed Tucker was in the driveway peering under the hood of a yellow Toyota Corolla. Sullivan had taken a statement from him on Friday and he confirmed Beatrice Pruitt's story regarding the events on Thanksgiving.

"If you're looking for Bea, she's inside. Maybe you could help me? Can you get in my car and turn on the engine and hit the gas when I give a signal?" He waved his hand in the air.

Sullivan followed directions and the Corolla started up after a few hits on the pedal.

"Thanks."

Beatrice was standing at the door to meet him. "I left the car door open by mistake and the overhead light must have drained the battery," she said. "Come in." On the chair in front of the television was the red felt jacket to a Santa suit and on an ironing board were the pants. She motioned to the couch for him to sit while she finished what she was doing.

"Ed's been hired as one of the Santas at the Wakefield Mall. He just took his suit out of storage and it needs a good pressing."

Tucker came in as she was putting the pants on a hanger with the jacket.

"Thanks, Bea. You're a pal." He patted her on the back. "Leave the motor running for a while and you should be okay. But I think you're gonna need a new battery soon. Gotta run and pick up the kids from the library," he explained.

After he'd left, Beatrice asked, "Can I get you something to drink, Detective?"

"No, I have some more interviews this morning."

She lowered herself into an overstuffed chair. The black patent leather ballerina shoes on her tiny feet barely touched the floor. "Do you have any leads on what happened to Sherman?"

"We're at the beginning of our investigation and still have a lot more information to compile, Mrs. Pruitt. I just need to ask you a few questions."

She sat up straighter on the edge of the chair, her small frame teetering forward. Sullivan suppressed an urge to push her back into the safety of the cushions.

"You said you open the store every morning. How many sets of keys do you have?"

"I've one key to the back door which leads into my office. That's how I usually get in. It's on a ring with another key I've never used. I don't even know what it's for. Luckily, I keep my spare key to the store's front door with me at all times. I put in my pocket when I leave the house for work each day."

"Which did you use on Friday morning?"

"I somehow misplaced my key ring. I unlocked the front door with the spare in my pocket."

"Does anyone else have keys?"

"Well, the owners and Deb, the manager. But like I told you Friday, the owners are skiing in Vermont and Deb flew to Virginia to spend Thanksgiving with her parents. Did Sherman get in with a key?"

"We found a key ring with two keys in his coat pocket and believe that's how he gained entrance, Mrs. Pruitt."

She let that sink in for a minute before she blurted out, "You don't think I gave him that key, do you?"

"I just spoke with Suzanne Tetreault. She lives in the apartment across from the store."

"Yes, my sister-in-law. I spoke with her yesterday after I got home from the police station."

Sullivan silently noted Tetreault had neglected to mention that. "She has custody of your son?"

"Buddy still lives with her. He has for a few years."

Sullivan waited for her to continue.

"He's been with her since before my divorce from Sherman. Buddy is my son from my first marriage. After my husband Daniel died, I found I couldn't take care of a baby, so he went to live with

Suzy until I got better. When I married Sherman, Buddy came to live with us for almost a year. But that didn't work out and he went back with his aunt. It was better for him there." Her head drooped as she brushed her fingers across her eyes.

"Well, thank you, Mrs. Pruitt. Please call if your key chain turns up or if you have any additional information that could help us." He handed her his card and she watched as he went down the front steps and out to his car.

Beatrice locked the door and went into the kitchen. On the table was a sheet of paper with the heading "to do list" and a pen. She took the pen and made a large X over the items then balled up the paper and threw it into the trash. She went to the cabinet under the sink and took out a bottle of vodka. Lowering herself slowly to the floor, she unscrewed the top and held it under her nose deeply inhaling the familiar scent that had kept her company for most of her adult life.

Vida Koransky had enough problems in her life without that jerk complicating it by getting himself killed. At the moment, she was supposed to be at the travel agent's making last minutes arrangements for her Caribbean cruise yet, here she was waiting for the cops to show up and grill her once again. What more could she add to what she'd told them last night? Sherman was a self-centered, boorish idiot and a mean drunk. He'd been renting a room from her and was behind on his payments. Now that he'd gotten himself murdered, she'd probably never see the money.

She'd already gathered up most of his belongings and placed them in garbage bags to give to his daughter. He had nothing of worth and if she'd found anything, she would have put it on e-bay to get back some of the money he owed her.

When they'd first met at the Alcoholics Anonymous meeting last summer, he seemed like a nice guy. He wasn't good looking. His nose was long and bulbous and his skin was pockmarked, but there was a charm about him. Some of her women friends described it as animal magnetism. They didn't live with him. He was an animal all right – a pig!

It wasn't long after he'd settled into her place that he began to show his true colors. On Thanksgiving he was watching football. He'd given her a subscription to the testosterone channel for her birthday and after that it was twenty-four hours of sports. He'd been drinking since he woke up and feelng brave, told her to go get him another brewsky. There already were five empty cans of beer on the side of his chair. She told him she was busy. He got up and grabbed the sheet of paper out of her hand and began reading out loud, mimicking her in a high pitched, whiney voice.

My Bucket List
Go on a cruise (someplace warm)
Treat myself to a spa day
Buy a car that's not a piece of junk
(blue Lincoln Continental?)
Join weight watchers and lose a few pounds
Get my GED

It didn't really bother her when he doubled over with laughter about her losing the weight.

"A few pounds? How about a ton?" But when he hooted, "You never graduated from high school? What a dummy!" She showed him the door and told him not to come back. She threw his winter jacket outside on the lawn and informed him she'd put the rest of his stuff out on the porch.

He threw the jacket into the back seat of the car and didn't bother to argue with her. He'd tried to bully her once, pushing her against the wall with his bloated belly. But she was a large woman and quick. She'd grabbed the cast iron frying pan from the stove and smashed him over the head. Luckily for him it was the small pan and not the one she used to make bacon in that morning. He knew enough not to challenge her. Even if he got a shot in while they were awake, he always fell asleep before her. She kept a copy of Faith McNulty's book, *The Burning Bed,* on her night table, just in case he forgot who was the boss in her house. If he even tried to mess with her, he'd go up in flames.

Sullivan stood looking at the four brown garbage bags over by the porch swing. A tube sock, a faded tee shirt and grey underpants had fallen out of one of them. He decided to leave them where they were and turned to ring the bell.

Vida Koranski took her time coming to the door. She'd made it clear to him on the phone she wasn't happy having to talk with the police twice.

"I answered all the questions Sergeant Carlyle asked. I got nothing more to tell you, Detective. Sherman only lived here for a few months and it was a few months too many."

"I have some things I'd like to clarify, Ms. Koransky. You could come down to the station if you'd like and we can talk there," he offered.

Sergeant Joanne Carlyle's description of Vida didn't do her justice. Sullivan had barely hidden his surprise when Koranski opened the door. The woman standing in front of him was at least six foot five and dressed in army fatigues. Large steel hoop earrings dangled from her ears and a nail stud pierced her upper lip. The middle finger of her right hand was covered by a gigantic black ring in the shape of a skull. Her lime green hair was loosely pulled back into a long, dangling ponytail tied with a bright pink bow. Under thick black brows, she squinted her wide, golden-flecked eyes. Looking him up and down, she stated in a deep, throaty voice, "You must be the cop."

"Detective Sullivan." He took out his badge, which she pointedly ignored.

"Come in."

She held the door open. He walked past her and noticed on her feet what his Nonni would have called "mules" - slippers with an opening to let the toes hang out. Vida's mules may, in the distant past, have been quite stylish but had been kept beyond their prime, obviously, for the sake of comfort. Only a remnant of orange feathers once glued to the tops could be detected. The faded leopard sateen material had long ago lost its shine. But the gigantic feet tucked into the mules were quite another story.

Tattooed vines covered every inch of skin. Ruby throated hummingbirds sipped from red tubular petals and Monarch butterflies danced along the dark green leaves. Each toenail was painted a different neon shade with silver glitter embedded in the polish. Turquoise, magenta, chartreuse, lilac, tangerine. It was a podiatric rainbow! He could hardly take his eyes from them.

"Sit down," Vida commanded, pointing to the couch. "I'll get you a coffee." She left the room for a minute, returning with a tray holding two mugs with the words Semper Fi encircling them. She offered him some cream in a pink panther pitcher.

"I take mine black, thanks."

"Exactly what is it you need to know that I haven't already told your sergeant?" she asked as she settled into a large, brown corduroy recliner.

It was times like this he missed Kara the most. She would have taken the lead and he would have been able to observe and record notes for them to discuss later. He took a gulp of coffee and cleared his throat. "You told Sergeant Carlyle you'd met Sherman Pruitt at an AA meeting back in the summer. Do you know if he continued to go to the meetings?"

"I'm sure he didn't. Sherman only went to those meetings to find himself a woman he could latch on to. He didn't have any intention of staying sober. Now me, I been sober for seven years, nine months, thirteen days."

He wasn't sure how to respond to this. Kara would have known exactly what to do. He nodded and cleared his throat again. "Do you know if he made any friends or enemies when he was going to the meetings?"

"Besides me, I don't remember him talking to anyone else. He met his first two wives at meetings. He told me that."

"Do you know either of them?"

"Never met the first one. But Beatrice I knew."

"Can you tell me anything about them?"

"The first wife died in a car crash. She got hit head on by a drunk driver. She was sober. How's that for irony?" She waited for Sullivan to say something and when he didn't she shrugged and went on. "They had a daughter, Evelyn. Lives up in Maine. I gave your sergeant the contact information and I called Evie to deliver the news of Sherman's passing."

"I've spoken with Evelyn on the phone. This morning."

"Then you know she'll be coming down to pick up his stuff and make the funeral arrangements. She hasn't spoke with her father in years. She was close to Beatrice's sister-in-law, Suzanne Tetreault. I expect that's where she'll be staying."

"And Mr. Pruitt had no other relatives?"

"None around here except for Bea. Poor Beatrice. He really messed up her life. Not that it wasn't already messed up before he showed up."

"Did you know he went to see her after he left your place on Thanksgiving?"

"No, I didn't. I don't know too much, but I can figure some things out. His body was found at Kenyon's and she's the manager there. Bea's a good person and she's had a lot of hard breaks in life. And the drinking's never helped."

"Do you know if Mrs. Pruitt still drinks?"

"Well, she's been trying to quit for years. She met Sherman at AA, like me. He hooked on to her real fast. A widow with a big insurance settlement. The only thing he wasn't happy about was the kid. And he made sure he got that little impediment taken care of pretty fast. Bea certainly has plenty of reason to want him dead."

"Might anyone else have similar feelings, Ms. Koranski?"

"Hell, I could make you a list. Have you talked with the lady principal, Rosa Brooks, at the school where he worked? I gave your sergeant Sherman's directory with all of the faculty's names and numbers."

"We've spoken with some of them already and intend to visit the school on Monday."

"You'll get an earful then. He certainly made that woman's life miserable whenever he got the chance. He'd come home bragging about stupid things he did to cause problems. Anything to interrupt the classes."

"Do you want to expand on that?"

"You're gonna see Ms. Brooks on Monday. I'm sure, if you ask the right questions, she'll tell you all about him. No love lost there and better to hear it from the horse's mouth."

Sullivan stood up. "Thank you for your help, Ms. Koranski. I'll certainly keep you informed of how the case is progressing."

"You don't have to bother. I'll read about it in the paper. Sherman's dead and that's all I need to know. Good riddance to bad rubbish, I say." She had slipped the mules off during the conversation and put them back on to walk him to the door.

Sullivan looked down again and wished his grandmother was still alive. He was going to phone Kara and tell her all about his meeting with Vida. He thought she'd get a chuckle out of it and it would be nice to hear her laugh. He'd call her when he got back to the office.

Sunday, November 26

3

How Lovely Are Your Branches

Stewart had made waffles in the shape of Christmas trees with mint sprinkles on top. He kept finding innovative ways to color his concoctions various shades of green. Avocados were a favorite additive much to Kara's dismay. She could still taste his guacamole and lime muffins weeks after he'd served them in honor of the Leonids Meteor Showers back in early November.

Her husband was a scientist who had a passion for experimenting with food. Since she was not really into cooking, the kitchen was his domain and the Christmas Season was ripe for his green, gastronomic concoctions. This morning he was wearing the apron she'd given him the first year they were married. On the front were the words:

We live on a blue planet
That circles around a ball of fire
Next to a moon that moves the sea
And you don't believe in Santa Claus?

Today they were going to decorate the house and in the evening, they'd put up the balsam fir they'd cut down on Saturday.

After breakfast Stewart went up to the attic to get the tree stand and the boxes of ornaments and lights. Sophia, Gino, Rick and Ruth were invited for dinner. Stewart had promised to make his famous green mashed potatoes au Tannenbaum with mushy peas and chicken breasts dipped in green ranch dressing and encrusted in panko crumbs. Kara had texted a warning to them tacking on numerous horrified-looking emojis. Ruth assured her that she and Rick would be bringing lots of hors d'ouevres for all of them to fill up on before sitting down to the meal.

"Kara, look what I found in one of the boxes." He entered the study with a pair of brown felt reindeer antlers and a large, stuffed, red nerf ball. "Remember when I bought these at Christmas Tree Shop three years ago? I surprised you and put them on the front of your car to make it look like you were driving behind Rudolph the red-nosed reindeer. I found them in a bin with the matching elf shoes I got for us. The ones with the curly toes and the bells." He shook the slippers and as the tinkling sound filled the room, he began to sing the store's signature, albeit repetitive, ditty, "Don't you just love a bargain? Don't you just love a bargain? Don't you just love a bargain? Don't you just …"

Kara glanced up from the mystery book she was reading and fearing the onset of an earworm, quickly interrupted the never-ending jingle loop. "The elf slippers! What a nice surprise!"

"I wondered where they'd disappeared to. Now what were they doing at the bottom of the bin with the Christmas linens?"

"I have no idea," Kara retreated back to her book and pretended to be focusing all her attention on the page she was reading.

"We'll have to be more careful this year when we pack them away. They should have their own special box – and I'll label it."

"Make sure you do that, Honey," Kara said, not looking up. She vividly remembered the last holiday season - driving her unmarked police car around with the antlers and reindeer nose stuck on the front grille. It was difficult to be unobtrusive that December, although Sullivan loved it and let her do all of the driving that month.

"Do you want another waffle? There are two more left."

"How about just a bit more tea?"

"Coming right up. I thought I heard your phone ringing a few minutes ago. I left a message for Ruth and Rick to come over early so I could try out my wintergreen stuffed mushrooms on them. Did she call back?"

"Oh, don't worry about hors d'oeuvres. They're bringing them. The call was from Carl Sullivan."

"Invite him over, too. Looks like we'll have plenty of food."

"He may stop by later. He's trying to spend some time with his family this morning, getting his own tree set up."

"Poor guy. I'll bet this will be a crazy Christmas for him with that murder case taking up his time." Stewart looked questioningly at his wife but she didn't return his gaze.

"Okay, well, I'll just take your cup and get you some more tea. Do you want me to add some flavor? I have lots of pesto left over …"

"It's fine. Your tea is always delicious straight up."

"Wait 'til you see the fruit punch I'm mixing together for tonight. Guess what color it's going to be?" He went off into the kitchen humming the jingle and doing a little jig.

Carl Sullivan took his family to the lot where the boy scouts were selling trees as a fundraiser. After much searching, examining and shaking of branches, they chose a Norfolk pine and tied it to the roof rack on top of their Subaru.

They picked up some donuts on the way home and his wife made hot chocolate for them as they untangled the lights from the heaps they'd been thrown in during the packing up last January. They never took the tree down before the Feast of the Epiphany on January 6th.

"I swear, Jess, we're going to pack everything up the right way this year. We're going to throw out all lights that don't work and wrap the good ones around a coat hanger so we don't spend half a day untangling them."

"You say that every year. I'll believe it when I see it," his wife said. "Hey, Connor, jelly donuts are for eating!"

By the time she got to the boy, who had a donut clutched in each tiny hand, it was too late. The two-year old had sprinkled powdered sugar on some of the lower branches and the dog was wildly licking the surrounding carpet.

"Snow, Mommy! Pretty snow."

"Yes, Darling, very lovely," his mother sighed as her husband chased the puppy, Max, around the coffee table and into the kitchen.

Connor's older brother got a towel and gently wiped the jelly from his sibling's hands and face. "I told you we should just get chocolate covered," he announced wisely to the adults in the room who, to Billy's unceasing dismay, had the power to make all the important decisions regarding food allowed in the house.

After the lights were up and the boys were hanging their favorite ornaments on the bottom branches, Carl put on his coat and gave his wife a kiss. "I've got to get over to the station and do some paperwork."

"This was nice. I'm glad Sergeant Shwinnard took over for you this morning. I'm sure everything's only going to get worse if you don't find the killer soon. Have you spoken with Kara?"

"We've talked. I'm going to call again when I get to the office and see if I can convince her to take a ride with me to interview a woman this afternoon."

"That would be a step in the right direction. You two are such a good team."

"I realized yesterday how much I miss having her in the room when I'm trying to get information from someone. She has a sixth sense. I've watched her. I sometimes think she can actually see through people. Especially if someone's telling lies."

"Imagine being married to a person like that," his wife teased him as she knotted the scarf hanging from his neck. "Stay safe." She kissed him on the lips. "See you tonight. Love you."

She stood watching him back his car out of the driveway. From the living room she heard the voices of her two boys.

"Bad doggy, Max!"

"Mommy, Mommy, Max is eating all of the candy canes we put on the tree. Come quick! He's throwing up on the couch!"

Sergeant Shwinnard was at his desk with Detective Brown reviewing the work they'd done so far when Sullivan came into the office. "Sad looking tree you've got there, Sergeant. Did you get a visit from the Grinch this morning?"

"Leo's been putting them on desks around the building. The tag says it's a miniature lemon cypress. Smells good! He picked up a bunch of them at Trader Joe's. There's probably one in your office. On a cheerier note, I've been reviewing all of these statements we have so far. And check out these pictures. Do you think it could have been an accident? Could Pruitt be a thief caught in the act? Was someone else with him and they had an argument?"

Sullivan scanned the photos of the scene. "At some point, we're led to believe Sherman Pruitt was involved in an altercation with someone. The spindle used to hold sales receipts was plunged into his neck, resulting in his death. He fell back against the mirror and then ended up on the floor of the dressing room. What else do we have?"

Shwinnard sorted through a folder and took out statements. "The key ring was found in his car inside a jacket pocket. That's how he entered the store. We don't know how the jacket and key ended up back in the car. Only three people had access to the back door keys. The owner was in Vermont. When I contacted him, he checked to make sure his keys were at his home where he left them in his wall safe. They were. The sales manager flew to Virginia for the holiday. She'll be back tonight. When we called her, she said she had her set right there with her."

"Beatrice Pruitt admitted she had the key on Wednesday morning when she opened up but misplaced it and had to let herself into the store on Friday with her front door key. I spoke with her again today and she still has no idea where the other key could be. I think we can safely presume it's the one we found in her ex-husband's jacket," Detective Brown said. "I asked her if he could have stolen it when he went by the house on Thursday. She said that was possible. But she told me he wasn't inside that long and she was with him all the time he was there. She seemed a little fuzzy on the details to me."

"I had an interesting conversation with Vida Koranski on Saturday. She mentioned Sherman met Beatrice and her at AA meetings. We'll call her in again when we have more details on what Pruitt was doing after he left her house. We need to find out what else he did in the intervening hours besides eat a Big Mac."

"We impounded his car He left it in the rear of the store parking lot, unlocked. There were empty beer cans on the floor, fast food wrappers on the passenger seat, and his jacket was in the back," Shwinnard said.

"Keep looking into this and interviewing people who might have been in town and seen him or his car that night. I'm going to visit the people he worked with." Sullivan took the school directory from the desk and put it in his pocket.

"Do you want someone on the team to go with you?"

"That's okay. I think I'll pay a visit to Detective Langley and see if she'd like to take a Sunday drive in the country."

Stewart was attempting to string lights on the holly bushes in front of the house when Carl Sullivan pulled into the driveway. "Long time, no see," he said.

"Let me give you a hand with that," Sullivan took some of the lights and began unraveling them, placing them in rows on the ground.

"Hey, you're good at this. We're decorating our Christmas tree later this evening. You could bring the wife and kids," Stewart offered.

Kara came down the steps and said in a tone, which Carl knew from experience to be her cautionary voice, "Yes, Stewart has some interesting recipes he'll be trying out on us." She whispered as she got into the car, "You may want to feed the boys first."

"Thanks, Stewart, but if I get some free time this evening, I'll finish decorating our tree. Connor and Billy can just about reach half way up so, until they grow some more, the top is my job. Maybe we'll stop by tomorrow night. The wife's working and I'm slated for babysitting duty."

"Sounds like a plan," Stewart waved to him as Carl shut the passenger door and went around to his side of the car.

"And I'm sure there'll be plenty of leftovers," Kara told him when he was behind the wheel.

Rosa Brooks was looking through the LL Bean catalogue. She'd decided to buy some evergreen wreaths and a small boxwood tree.

For the first time in three years, she had reason to celebrate. Sherman Pruitt was dead. The fact that he'd been murdered did not make the man any less odious. She wondered to herself just how much she should share with the police as she heard the car outside.

When the bell rang, she closed the catalogue and opened the door. For a moment, she stood silent. She'd been expecting Detective Sullivan, but the black woman next to him took her by surprise.

"Kara! How nice! I wasn't expecting you. I haven't seen you at any of our meetings lately."

"Hello, Rosa. I'm here unofficially with Detective Sullivan."

"Yes, I'd heard you were on leave. I'm really glad to see you. Come on in." She led them both into her study. "I can get you some tea or coffee or a cold drink, if you'd like?"

"Tea would be fine, Rosa," Kara said. "Would you like me to help you?"

"No, the kettle's whistling, so I just have to put another mug on the tray. Detective, what can I get you?"

"I'll have tea, thank you, Ms. Brooks."

When she left the room, Sullivan looked at his old partner. "You didn't mention you knew her when I asked you to come along."

"I'm full of surprises. Rosa and I serve together on a board - black women concerned with the rising incarceration rate of young black men. When you told me who you'd be interviewing, I thought I might be of help. Rosa is trustworthy and she can be extremely outspoken at times. But I'm not sure how open she'd be with a white cop."

Sullivan thought about this, "Good to know. I wondered why you'd agreed to come along."

"Well, escaping from Stewart's cooking and serenading for a while was a major part of the plan. And I really hate stringing lights. It is a situation ripe for ending in a family argument."

"I hear you."

Rosa returned with a tray and sat on the couch next to Kara.

"Ah, sugar cookies! And they're not green." Kara sighed in relief.

Rosa offered, "I have some Oreos with mint green filling if you'd like?"

"Oh, no, these look delicious," Kara assured her. Sullivan chuckled.

"I suppose you have some questions about Sherman Pruitt, Detective?"

"We're investigating his murder and trying to find out what he did in the hours and days before his death on Thursday," Sullivan explained."

"Well, he certainly didn't come in to work," she said. "He was fired over a month ago."

"Could you tell us what led to his firing?"

"I could give you many reasons, Detective. Getting caught with a bag of cash in his office and a young woman he shouldn't have been with were just the latest in his seemingly never-ending infractions."

"I take it the money was not his?"

"It was cash that should have been deposited in the school accounts from a fund raiser in September. In addition to discipline and supplies, school accounts was one of the responsibilities Superintendent Harknettal assigned to Sherman."

"And the young woman? Was she a student?"

"No, I would have reported that immediately. She was an office aide. And they were both very scantily dressed for this time of year, if you get my drift."

"Ms. Brooks, could I ask how someone like Sherman could have been hired by your school department?"

"I suggest you take that up with our superintendent, Mr. Harknettal. He and Sherman were buddies from way back."

"What was it like working with him?" Kara asked.

"He made my job even more difficult, if that's even possible. I found nothing redeeming about him. An ape of a man stalking around the halls of the school, storming into classrooms. When I first came upon him peeping through the window of a classroom door, I thought to myself, we need to put a poster over the inside of that opening."

"Why was he hired, Rosa? Didn't you have anything to say about who you'd be working with?"

"Hah! Principals in this state have no say in anything. We don't even have a union. Superintendents, school committees, teachers' unions - NEA, AFT - they all have a say. But the person in charge of the running of the school every day, what do we know?"

"So, he was hired without your okay?"

"I really needed an assistant, having run the school for two years on my own. With little money in the budget, he was the best this small district could muster. The school board knew he'd been tossed out of a couple of schools. They didn't care. He was recommended by the superintendent and he came cheap. That's always been the bottom line for them."

"It sounds like a stressful situation for you. Wasn't there anyone who'd listen?" Kara asked, placing her hand on her friend's arm.

"I was secretly warned ahead of time about keeping an eye on him around the younger, female staff. A woman administrator who had the dubious pleasure of working with him in another district called to give me a heads up. He'd earned quite a reputation before he arrived. She let me in on all of his little tricks, so I wasn't blindsided when he tried them out here."

"And now you'll be on your own again," Detective Sullivan said.

"Being on my own actually comes as a relief. I'll gladly accept the extra hours and the added paperwork not to have the burden of babysitting for a bully who used his large belly as a bulldozer. More than once, I'd found him cornering an unfortunate woman against a wall, invading her space with garlicky words shouted into her face. I'd tried to convince them to file charges against him with their union. They brushed it all off with, 'That's just Sherman being Sherman.' He seemed to be able to psyche out the gullible ones who found his macho behavior irresistible. I know there are naïve women like that, but it still is beyond my comprehension why anyone would put up with the mental and emotional abuse this type of guy doles out."

"And who finally caught him in flagrante?" Sullivan asked.

"That would be our new assistant superintendent. He was hired at the beginning of the school year."

"Why would anyone listen to him, if they didn't listen to you?" Sullivan asked.

"Dr. Cranmore is politically connected and he's a man," Rosa Brooks turned and nodded to Kara who nodded back.

"Thanks for being so frank with us. I'll be coming by the school tomorrow to speak with some of the teachers," Sullivan said.

"You can use my office for your interviews. And if you would bring Kara with you, that would be most appreciated."

Darkness was setting in. Stewart turned on the outdoor decorations. The tree was already in its stand in the middle of the room. Lights were strewn in bunches over the backs of chairs and on the floor.

"Shouldn't we at least try to untangle them?" Kara asked.

"Gino will have them straightened out in no time when he gets here," her husband assured her. "Do you remember where I put those elf slippers? I was hoping we could both wear them tonight."

"I thought I last saw them in the dining room. Could you have moved them somewhere when you brought the ornament boxes down?"

"I'll just look upstairs. I'll be right back. Don't bother doing anything with those lights."

"No worries there, Sweetie," she said, mostly to herself, as she turned on the candles in the windows. Headlights shone into the room. "They're here," she called up to her husband.

Friends poured into the kitchen. They placed platters of food on the kitchen counter tops. Rick collected their coats to hang in the hall closet. Ruth began to uncover the dishes. "I can assure you, there is nothing green under that tinfoil," she whispered to Kara and Sophia.

Gino lowered himself gingerly into the rocking chair in front of the fireplace in the dining room. "Ahhhhh! Ohhhhhhhh!"

"You just stay right there, Honey. I'll get you a nice cold beer," Sophia patted the top of his head as he gave a series of short grunts.

Stewart joined them, "Hello!" He hugged Ruth and Sophia and shook Rick's hand. I can't find the elf slippers anywhere," he told his wife.

"Don't worry, I'm sure they'll show up when you least expect it." She kissed him on the cheek.

"The food's all ready. We can eat before we decorate the tree," he announced.

Gino groaned.

Kara pulled Rick aside. "What's the matter with your brother?"

"He's on strike."

Sophia brought her husband a beer, "My poor baby," she kissed his forehead, "He's been helping me all day. He put up the tree in the children's ward at the hospital. Then he had to get all of the decorations out of storage at the Courthouse Center and when he got home he helped me with the trees at our house," Sophia announced.

"One for every room," Gino moaned.

They all looked at Gino and nodded sympathetically.

"Does this mean you won't be helping me with the lights?" Stewart asked.

Gino looked to his twin for help.

"This might be a good time to tell them about the Jewish side of the family. I'll bet Aunt Greta's menorahs are looking pretty good to you right now, bro." Rick gave his brother another beer.

Buddy could hear his aunt snoring softly as he walked past her bedroom. Outside on the sidewalk, he pulled the hood up over his head. Snow coated his jacket as he walked up the hill.

A tree had been set in his mother's living room window. It brought back memories. Sitting on the stonewall fronting the woods across from her house, he watched as the two children hung ornaments on the branches. A man lifted a small boy as he reached to put a star on the top. Buddy remembered that star. The tree suddenly lit up, casting colors out into the front yard.

He sat a while longer watching the celebration happening inside. Once, he thought he'd caught a glimpse of Santa Claus. The kids were gleefully jumping up and down next to the tree. Standing up, he shook the snow from his sleeves and turned to walk back down the hill.

Monday, November 27

4

OUR FINEST GIFTS WE BRING

Carl Sullivan kept looking over the evidence the team had gathered during the past few days. Everything pointed in the direction of Beatrice Pruitt. He'd asked Kara's advice and she'd cautioned him to wait until he had all the facts on his desk before making an arrest.

"You need to keep all avenues open. Often it does end up being the most obvious conclusion but sometimes a case needs to play out for a while before the actual culprit is sussed out," she'd told him.

Leo appeared at the door, "Evelyn Pruitt is here. Miss Pruitt, this is Detective Sullivan."

The young woman entered Sullivan's office and he stood to greet her. "I know you're busy and I appreciate your stopping in Miss Pruitt. Please accept my condolences on the loss of your father." He pulled a chair up to the front of his desk for her to take a seat.

"Thank you, Detective Sullivan. Please call me Evelyn."

"Would you like tea or coffee?"

"No, I have some matters to attend to. I was just at Vida's house and collected my father's belongings. She said you'd met with her Saturday, so you're aware I haven't spoken with my father for quite some time."

"Ms. Kowalski informed us of your situation. Could I ask the reason for your estrangement?"

"My father was a horrible person. He preyed upon women and had no respect for anyone unless he thought he could get something from them. I'm sure Vida gave you a full picture of exactly who he really was."

"Ms. Kowalski did tell me a bit about her experience with your father, but it appeared to me he'd met his match in her."

"You're right, Detective. He totally underestimated her when they first met. But that wasn't the case with my mother or his second wife, Beatrice."

"Vida said your mother had died in an accident."

Evelyn looked down at the bag in her lap and Carl waited for her to answer.

"My father found my mother at a meeting for people who had problems with alcohol. He figured out pretty soon that her parents had money. She was naïve and vulnerable. She ended up pregnant with me and they were married. My grandparents had to sign for her. She was younger than I am now. I don't remember much because she died when I was seven."

"Ms. Koranski told me it was a drunk driver."

"Did she tell you that we were with my grandparents when she got the call to pick him up?"

"She didn't mention he was in the car. She just said your mother was driving."

"He'd been at a sports bar watching a Patriot's football game with some other guys. He was so drunk, he blacked out. His buddies had to carry him to the car and strap him in the front seat. My mom had borrowed my grandparent's car to get him. They were hit just outside the bar by one of the other fans who'd been celebrating the Pats' win. My mother was killed instantly. My father ended up with a split lip and a few bruises."

"It must have been difficult for you, growing up without your mom."

"I moved to Maine with my grandparents not long after he married Bea."

"I've spoken with her. It appears she had some difficult years with him."

"She married him because she thought he would understand. Her husband was killed in a hit-and-run accident. They never caught the person responsible. Dad met her at an AA meeting, too. Once he found out there was insurance money to be had, he knew he'd found his next wife."

"Did he receive any money from your mother's accident?"

"My grandfather made sure there was a pre-nup. He'd taken out the insurance. Everything she had went to me."

"Did you get along with Beatrice?"

"She cared for me like I was her real daughter which would have been fine if he wasn't living in the house with us. Bea made sure Buddy and I were safe with her husband's sister. Whenever my father went on a binge, she'd take us for a walk down to Sue's and we'd stay there for the night."

"He was violent?"

"He broke things and would lash out if you got in his way. She knew the warning signs and made sure we were away from the house by then."

"Why didn't she call the police?"

"Bea was never assertive. She was a fractured human being. And she drank to forget. She was afraid to report him. He told her she was a drunk and she'd be in trouble, too, and she'd lose her son."

"But she did report him. We have it on file."

"After I went to live in Maine and Buddy was with Suzanne, Bea sobered up and found help at the Women's Resource Center in town. That gave her the courage to call the cops, and toss him out, and to finally divorce him."

"Evelyn, did your stepmother ever fight back when your father was in a rage?"

"Bea's a gentle soul. But there was one time when I saw her angry. I had been playing with a trophy on the bureau and dropped it. When my dad found his precious award broken, he went into a rage. He asked me who did it and I told him it was Buddy. Bea was giving Buddy a bath and he came roaring into the bathroom and pushed the boy's head under water. He'd done this before but this time she was terrified he was going to drown her son. She grabbed a pair of scissors and stabbed my father in the neck."

Sullivan was stunned by this piece of information. He stood up. "I appreciate your time, Evelyn. I'll notify you when we have further information on who murdered your father."

"Thank you. I'll be staying with Suzanne for a few days. Oh, I almost forgot …" she opened her bag and handed him a package wrapped in brown paper and tied with a red twine.

After she'd left, he untied the string and opened the gift. It was a box of fruitcake cookies. A Christmas card with a soft watercolor of a woman and a boy pulling a sled bearing a tree, a dog following behind them, opened to reveal a note:

Made with love,
Buddy and Suzy.

He smiled, putting the present back into its wrapper and placing it next to the miniature Grinch tree on his desk.

Ruth walked around the house, amazed at the decorations. "Sophia you really do have a tree in every room! No wonder Gino refused to lift a hand last night."

"Oh, he was just tired and cranky - low blood sugar. He adores celebrating the holidays."

In the living room, in front of the picture window was an eight-foot aluminum tree covered with vintage mercury glass bulb ornaments. A rotating light in one corner was positioned to reflect on the branches and change the colors of the tree every twenty seconds. "This was my grandmother's tree. They were popular back in the '60s. I found it in my parents' attic. And I think the ornaments belonged to my great grandmother. Gino found the light at a garage sale and brought it home to me for a Valentine's gift last year. He's so romantic."

On the kitchen table was a rosemary tree with red bows tied to each end. Ruth pinched the tips and the pungent scent of the herb filled the air.

"Rosemary, that's for remembrance," Sophia whispered.

In the master bedroom a green, goose feather tree with a pink satin cherub perched on the top sat in the middle of a round table by a window. "This belonged to my Great Aunt Sophia. I was named after her. She brought it to America when she emigrated from Germany. The first artificial Christmas trees. They were very popular there when people were concerned about deforestation back in the early 1900's."

"I've seen them for sale in high-end gift shops. They were quite expensive. I can't imagine what this antique must be worth."

"I would never sell it. I have such lovely memories of my aunt every time I see it. According to my father, she had quite a personality. He used to tell me I was just like her."

The aroma of a live Norway spruce permeated the air in the dining room. Something in the tree flickered. Ruth moved in closer. Enlaced within the branches were silky cobwebs. A large glass spider sat at the top, its glistening eyes looking down on the room below.

"In Germany, finding a spider or a web in a tree is believed to be good luck. Every Christmas Eve, my Aunt Sophia would tell us a folk tale about a poor widow and her children. One day, a pinecone lodged in the dirt floor of their hut. They let it grow, but when it became a tree, they could not afford decorations. When they awoke on Christmas, the morning sun reflected off all of the webs that had covered the tree in the night, turning them to gold and silver. Gino never gets tired of my telling him the story. He brings me a fresh–cut tree on the Saturday after Thanksgiving every year."

They went upstairs to Sophia's art studio. On a podium in the center of the room was a homemade ceramic tree sculpture with lights emanating through holes shaped like tiny stars. Sophia closed the shades and the effect was magical. "This one I created myself," she informed her friend. "I'll make you one if you'd like."

"I would love to have a Christmas tree made by you. I would leave it out all year round."

"There's one more for you to see."

A pinecone tree filled with colorful birds sat by the hearth in the den and bird songs filled the room. "Gino made this one for me on our first Christmas together. It's my favorite."

Little Charley Brown branches were tied together with twine and scattered around on the windowsills in the room. On the floor were presents wrapped in paper designed with pictures of birds, feathers, angels, pinecones, stars, and spider webs. Ruth was enraptured by the scene.

"Sophia, where did you find time to buy these presents? And they're all done up so beautifully!"

"Oh, I shop for special things all year long. When I see something that someone I know would like, I buy it to stash away in my gift closet." She opened a double door to reveal boxes and bags on the shelves. "I've already begun next year's shopping. Now let's sit down and make sure we have everything set for your wedding."

"Sophia, I have no doubt with you in charge everything will be perfect," her future sister-in-law said.

Kara handed Sullivan the shopping bag. "Happy Holidays!"

He peeked inside. "Wow! My very own reindeer antlers and Rudolph's nose. I should put these on the car now."

"No! Wait 'til later," she said grabbing his arm as he started to open the door. Stewart waved at them from the porch.

"Okay. What are these?"

"Elf shoes. I thought the boys might enjoy them."

"They're great! And I didn't bring you anything," he said.

"Trust me, your happiness and the smile on your face is the only gift I need."

"Speaking of smiles, I forgot to tell you. I spoke with Sherman Pruitt's girlfriend, Vida Koranski. The woman he was staying with before she kicked him to the curb. You'd have loved her."

Sullivan told her all about the interview and Kara laughed, declaring this was a woman after her own heart. She admitted to herself how much she missed working with her old partner.

When they arrived at the school, the bell had just rung signaling a change of classes. Teenagers filled the corridors as Kara and Carl stood watching while lockers banged and bodies jostled each other in the four minutes to get from one class to another. They inched their way through the throng and into the main office.

Five students sat dejectedly on the chairs lined up outside the door to the vice principal's office. Principal Brooks came out and told the woman at the desk to give them all a pass to their next class. When they'd gone on their way, the secretary shook her head as four more students were sent in from the next class by the same teacher. Brooks glanced at their discipline slips and told them to take out their books and read quietly until the next class.

"Goosenik's on a tear today! What should I do if she sends more students from class? We're running out of chairs," the secretary whispered.

"Send a sub to cover her class. We'll conduct the interview with Ms. Goosenik first." She wrote a quick note to have the sub give to the teacher. "Detective Sullivan, Kara, so nice to see you again. This is my hard-working, underpaid secretary, Sandra Wallace." She smiled at them over a desk piled high with paperwork. "Sandy has the list of teachers you mentioned you wanted to see. She'll send for them when you're ready."

The office was a small space with unpainted cinder block walls, but sun streamed through a window in the back of the room. "Here's a copy of the list of people you requested to see - unfortunately, two of my staff have taken an extra vacation day. But the others have been informed of your visit and are more than willing to speak with you about Sherman. You're welcome to use my office for as long as you need it. I spend most of my day out in the corridors and classrooms, anyhow. Please tell Sandy to call if you need me." She pointed to the walky-talky on her belt.

There was a knock on the door and Rosa Brooks let in a large woman who seemed to be out of breath. "Detectives Sullivan and Langley, this is Lucille Goosenik."

The woman pushed right past Brooks, throwing her fleshy body into the closest chair. Kara and Sullivan glanced at each other and then quickly looked away, both thinking the same thing: *Lucy Goosenik - the kids must have a field day with that name!*

"Ms. Goosenik, thank you for coming in to speak with us about Mr. Pruitt."

She wriggled a bit farther back in her seat, "Please call me Lucy. I was a very good friend of Sherman. I don't know what we'll do without him." She yanked a Kleenex from the cuff of her sleeve and dabbed daintily at her eyes, then wiped the sweat from her forehead and chin.

Sullivan gave her time to compose herself and before continuing, "We're very sorry for your loss."

"Sherman was a kindred spirit. He understood how frustrating it can be for an educator of my caliber to have to teach students who just don't want to learn. Now, my own children are in a private school where the students truly want to learn. The tuition is steep but well worth the opportunity for them to have friends from a higher economic strata."

Kara stared at the woman sitting across from her and almost said something, but decided to sit back and wait to see what else would come from this person's mouth. She stifled an urge to go out into the office and pat each of Goosenik's students on the back to console them and assure them things can only get better.

Sullivan continued, "Since you were such good friends, could you tell us if Mr. Pruitt ever discussed problems he may have been having with anyone?"

She swiped at the sweat on her upper lip. Her eyes widened. "Sherman didn't have problems with anyone. You know he was fired last month? You should look into that. We all loved him. I think it was a sin. A real sin! I'm glad teachers have a union. Let them try to fire us! Humph!"

"Do you feel Mr. Pruitt should not have been fired?"

"Anyone who knows Sherman understands he's an extremely attractive man. That young woman set him up. Mark my words! He was trapped."

"And what about the cash found in his office?"

"Have you met his secretary? Gloria Pinto. She's the person they should have fired. Gloria's job is to deposit any funds he gives her into the accounts. Sherman probably didn't even know the money was still in his file cabinet."

"Did he have a good relationship with Mrs. Pinto?"

"Mrs.? Gloria isn't married. She had three kids by different men. But they never married her," she nodded imperiously.

Sullivan persisted, "What kind of relationship did she have with Mr. Pruitt?"

"Oh, she was very loyal to Sherman. She actually loved all of the men in the school. But she hated the women. She even refused to talk with some of us. A strange duck, that one."

"So, except for the members of the school committee who fired him and the young woman who set him up, you can't think of anyone else who had a problem with Mr. Pruitt?" Sullivan made eye contact with her and held it.

She wriggled uncomfortably in her chair and wiped her palms with the now shredded Kleenex. "Everyone adored Sherman. I'm sure there's been a mistake. It must have been an accident."

"Thank you, Ms. Goosenik. We'll be in touch if we have any more questions."

Kara fought the urge to continue questioning her so that her students could have more time with the substitute, but she remained silent as the woman left the office. Sullivan went out to ask Sandy if Mr. Sherman's secretary was available.

"Ms. Pinto isn't here. She's in court today."

"In court?"

"Yes, she attacked a woman who was in front of her in the express lane at the supermarket. The woman had more than twelve items, so she hit her over the head with a frozen turkey."

He sighed. "Please send in the next teacher on the list." He returned to the office where Kara was standing looking out the window to the yard below.

"This place is full of looneys!"

"Did you like school?" she asked him without turning around.

"I went to parochial school. The nuns could be tough on the boys. But I was a pretty good student, so I stayed out of trouble. Plus, my

55

parents would have killed me if I'd come home with a discipline note from one of the good sisters. What about you?"

"Let's just say it was not the best time in my life. I got bored easily and tended to go off on my own. Some of my teachers weren't comfortable with that. I spent a lot of time in the office. But luckily, my principal was kind. She used to give me things to do for her instead of leaving me sitting out on the bench. She had a table behind her desk filled with books. She collected illustrated children's books and actually had some with black characters. I think she may have bought them just for me. She let me take them home and said I didn't have to bring them back. They were the most cherished gifts I've ever received. She sends me a letter every Christmas. She's retired but still working with kids." Kara turned as the next teacher entered the room.

"Detectives Langley and Sullivan, this is Marylyn Shiffley. She's a first year math teacher." Sandy left Shiffley with the two detectives. Kara nodded and sat on the window ledge while Sullivan began the questions.

"I was informed by Principal Brooks that you'd come to her in regard to a situation involving Mr. Pruitt. Could you tell us about the incident?"

"It wasn't just one time, actually it was a series of incidents. I brushed off the first few times, thinking Mr. Pruitt was trying to joke with me. He told me I was too serious and should loosen up a bit." She stopped talking. Sullivan waited. "I noticed him looking in the window of the classroom door. He seemed to be there every class, but he didn't come in. Just stood out in the corridor gawking. I finally went to the door and asked if he would like to come inside and join the class. And he did. He sat in the back of the class playing with his iPhone. Afterwards, he told me he was taking notes for my teacher evaluation. I went to Ms. Brooks and she advised me to speak with my union rep about being evaluated without prior notice. My union rep explained the proper procedure. He must have spoken with Mr. Pruitt because there was a change in his behavior toward me." She stopped again and Sullivan took out his cell.

"I need to answer this text," he explained and excused himself from the room leaving her alone with Kara to continue the interview.

"Marylyn, how do you like teaching?" Kara sat down next to her.

"Oh, I really love it. The kids are fantastic and I've always wanted to be in my own classroom. And I even get to have an after-school club. I'm adviser of the junior debate group," she said proudly.

"Can you explain what you meant about Mr. Pruitt's change in behavior? What did he do differently?"

"Well, before, he seemed a bit flirty. But after that incident, he seemed hostile. He would come charging into the room and interrupt my classes. He'd ignore me and call on individual kids, asking innocuous questions - if they were going to the football game or if they were getting enough homework. He'd get them to yell and cheer and then he would abruptly leave me to settle them back to their class work."

Sullivan returned with a bottle of water for each of them, standing aside to let Kara continue the interview with the young woman.

"Once, when I was in the office after school checking my mailbox, he snuck up behind me and pushed his stomach against me. Ms. Brooks came in and he moved away. But she called me into the office and we spoke. I explained what had been going on. She told me she was writing up a report and was going to speak with Mr. Porthull. He teaches in the science department and he's also a union rep. She also explained that she would be handling my evaluation, not Mr. Pruitt."

Kara was curious. "Did this help alleviate the problem?"

"Mr. Pruitt stopped barging into my class and everything appeared to be okay until after school one night, when the debate club had left and I was at my desk correcting some papers, Mr. Pruitt came in. He stood in front of the door and just glared at me. I felt cornered. He seemed to be enjoying making me uncomfortable."

"Did he say anything to you?" Kara asked.

"He started to walk toward me and that was when the principal came in. She had her cell phone out and I think she may have had the videotape on. She told him to meet her in the office. Ms. Brooks apologized to me and said it would be taken care of. She walked me to my car and told me not to worry that she'd been getting a lot of positive feedback from the students and parents about what a great job I was doing. She said she was looking forward to being at the next debate."

"And what happened after that?"

"Mr. Pruitt stayed away from me and then I heard he'd been fired. I asked Ms. Brooks if it was because of me and she reassured me he'd been heading toward dismissal for a long time. I was relieved but when I found out he was dead, I felt bad for him."

"We appreciate your speaking with us. We're trying to find out more about Mr. Pruitt and this has been a help," Kara assured the young woman.

After she'd left, Sullivan looked at the list. "Most of these people have already been interviewed, but I would like to speak with Porthull, the union rep and get his take on the situation."

Sandy knocked on the door. "Mr. Porthull is on his way and Superintendent Harknettal just called. He said to inform you he'll be leaving at two-thirty today." It was almost two. They thanked Sandy for relaying the message.

"He said he might have a few minutes to give you on Tuesday morning," she added before closing the door.

When the secretary was out of the room Sullivan said, "Oh, he'll give me a few minutes, all right - in my office at the station." Kara chuckled.

Aside from his beady eyes, Steven Porthull was a somewhat attractive man. His blond hair was thinning, but he carried himself well and wore a suit and tie. Most of the teachers appeared to dress casually, but perhaps his position as a union leader required more formal attire. Kara stood as he entered and moved back to the window. He shook hands with Sullivan and nodded to Kara when introduced.

"Terrible thing, this murder. Sherm was a good guy. Very popular. I can't imagine anyone wanting him dead. Do you have any suspects?"

Sullivan decided to take control of the questions. "We were hoping to get a feel for the victim and the people he knew before narrowing the field of suspects. How did you get along with him, Mr. Porthull?"

"I liked the guy. He never gave me any trouble. He was in charge of assigning duty periods and he always made sure I had a study hall in my own classroom so I could get all my paperwork done at my own desk. He did my evaluations and I always ended up with an A+ on everything. As a union person, I prefer having a man do the evaluations. Women can tend to be sticklers, if you know what I mean."

Sullivan glanced at Kara who remained poker-faced over by the window.

"Speaking of the weaker sex," Sullivan purposely didn't look over at Kara for her reaction, "it's come to my attention Mr. Pruitt had problems in regard to some of the younger female faculty. Were you aware of any matters we should know about?"

"Sherm was a single guy. He appreciated an attractive woman. He had a few misunderstandings with some of the newer teachers, but all of that was straightened out."

"Ms. Brooks seems to feel the incidents were more than just misunderstandings."

"And where did that get her?" he snarled. "If she'd stayed out of it and let the union handle it, Sherm would still be on the job and she wouldn't be stuck all by herself running this place, now would she?"

Kara had taken a real dislike to this man and stepped forward. Sullivan understood her intent and let her continue with the interrogation.

"So you had a good relationship with Mr. Pruitt for the entire time he was an administrator here?" Kara asked him.

"I would definitely say we had a great relationship. Sherm was a man's man in my book."

"Not to be too much of a stickler, Mr. Porthull, but you were aware his contract had not been renewed at his previous school. Do you have any idea why he was let go?" She'd taken out a folder from her briefcase and began to remove pages.

Porthull loosened his collar a bit. "Well, there were allegations of some improprieties and the school committee didn't really understand the job of an administrator. You know principals don't have union protection. They serve at the whim of the superintendent and if he tells the school committee he wants a principal out, then the poor guy is shown the door."

"So, you're telling me your friend Sherman was let go because of false allegations? Wouldn't he have a right to a hearing?"

"Yes, but he decided not to inconvenience people with hearings. Teachers would have to be brought in as witnesses - and parents. It was the assistant superintendent who reported him, you know. Sherm had a great relationship with Superintendent Harknettal and Sherm knew he'd lined up another job for him."

"Appears like there's a real 'Good Ole Boy Club' going on in some places, Mr. Porthull. I was wondering, as a union leader, if you realize that 73% of teachers are women? And most administrators are men. Seems a bit out of whack to me, wouldn't you say?" She turned her back on Porthull, not waiting for confirmation.

Sullivan dismissed the man, leading him out the door. "Thank you for your help. We'll be in touch if we have further questions."

When he returned he asked, "It looks like you've done some research on our victim's past? We should have an interesting conversation in the car on the way home."

Rosa Brooks met them as they were leaving her office. She'd been helping students put up a large artificial tree in the vestibule. They were hanging hand-made construction paper boxes on the branches.

"The Giving Tree," she explained. "Inside each small box, the students are placing messages bearing the name of a child, their age, and a gift they would like to receive from Santa. The gifts will be delivered to the local Johnnycake Center for the families who are having difficulties during this holiday season."

The two detectives looked at the messages being assembled on the table. Sullivan asked if he could take one for a young boy who wanted a football. "I'll buy it tonight and get it to you this week," he told Rosa.

Kara stared at the paper in her hand:

Jolene, age 7.
I would like a jewelry box. One that plays music, please.

She carefully placed the request in her pocket, thinking of the enameled box she'd been given, which now sat on the night table. She wound the key on the bottom every evening and listened to the "Ode to Joy" before she went to sleep. The tune reminded her of the person who had died on her watch and she was determined the young woman's memory would continue. Tonight, she would wrap up the music box for Jolene.

Tuesday, November 28

5

You Have Termites in Your Smile, Mr. Grinch

Early the next morning, Carl Sullivan placed a call to Superintendent Harknettal's office informing him he was expected to come to the station to be interviewed in regard to the murder of Sherman Pruitt.

"I couldn't p-possibly be there today. I'm a b-busy m-man," he huffed into the phone.

"We had an appointment with you yesterday that you chose not to keep. You can drive yourself to the station or I can send a squad car to pick you up." Grudgingly Harknettal agreed to be there around ten.

Sullivan called Kara to ask if she'd like to sit in on the interview.

"I'd planned to go by Kenyon's and speak with Beatrice Pruitt this morning, like we discussed. I'll stop at the station when I'm done."

The store was eerily quiet when Kara entered through the front door and strode toward the office. A few people milled around the accessories counter and a clerk was arranging bibs and rattles in a basket on a table in the infant's department, but the silence and the greyness of the day cast a pall over the large, open space.

Beatrice Pruitt was in her office speaking to a tall, gaunt man in a tan trench coat. They were having a heated conversation. His face was beet red, like that of a petulant child holding its breath, Kara thought. She moved to a nearby counter and busied herself looking at men's accessories.

She thought about buying a bow tie for Stewart, but swiftly nixed the idea. Stewart loved to mimic accents and she feared a bow tie might spur him to take on the persona of some famous bow-tie wearers like Winston Churchill, Groucho Marx or Pee Wee Herman. Then a horrific picture flashed across her mind - Stewart doing an impression of Jerry Lewis in *The Nutty Professor*. This gift potentially could be a total disaster. The decision was made. Her husband would not be getting a bow tie this Christmas.

Suddenly her thoughts were interrupted when she heard the man in the office snarling. Kara saw spittle came from his contorted mouth as he leaned in closer to Beatrice. "Don't th-th-think ya-ya-you're going to g-g-get away wi-with th-th-this!"

"I honestly don't know what you're talking about," she pleaded with the irate person towering over her.

He pounded on the file cabinet next to him and pointed his finger in the frightened woman's face. "Open it!"

Kara moved quickly into the room, stepping between them, forcing him to move back.

"You should leave," she said staring him down. He looked past her and shook his fist at the pale, quaking figure cringing behind this imposing black woman.

He didn't get any words out of his mouth before Kara warned, "I won't tell you again. Leave."

The ominous tone of her voice caused him to reassess his behavior. Whatever he was going to say, he decided it was better to remain silent. Brushing past the two women, he left the office. They watched as he rushed down the center aisle. He turned around once, as if to come back, but when he saw that Kara had her cell phone in hand, he thought better of it and ran from the store.

Beatrice straightened up, placing her right hand on the desk to steady herself. She dropped wearily into the chair and sat staring at the floor. Kara closed the door and waited until the ashen-faced woman finally looked up at her.

"Do you know that man?"

"I've never seen him before in my life. I thought he might be a new sales rep or buyer. He just came barging in here demanding I give him the folder. And something about a key. He went over to the file cabinet and tried to open it, but I hadn't unlocked it this morning."

"Did he give you his name or show some form of identification?"

"Nothing. He'd only been here a few minutes before you arrived."

"Did he say anything else to you?"

Beatrice shook her head.

A clerk knocked on the door and interrupted them "That man stopped at my counter and asked if the woman in the office was Bea Pruitt and I told him she was. He was very quiet and spoke in a whisper. He looked like one of the salesmen who come by all the time. I'm really sorry, Ms. Pruitt, if I caused a problem."

"You did nothing wrong, Sherry. It's okay." The clerk left.

Kara sat down on the other side of the desk. "You've never seen nor spoken with that man before?"

"Never. I would have remembered him, I'm sure."

"Could you open the file drawers to check and see if everything's in order?"

Beatrice put her hand into one of the desk's many cubbyholes and took out a small key, which she used to open the cabinet. "Nothing appears to be out of order."

Kara stood next to her looking into the top drawer. "Please open the others and tell me if you notice anything different from the last time you worked with the files." She watched as Beatrice went through, opening folders, inspecting contents.

"Nothing is out of place. I can't imagine what could be so important to him or anyone, for that matter. We keep invoices, receipts, cashed checks, resumes, ads - just regular every-day business papers. I do all of the filing, myself. If he'd asked for something specific, I could have looked into it for him, but he seemed to take it for granted I knew exactly what he wanted."

"If he returns or gets in touch, call the police immediately. I'm going to the station now and I'll give Detective Sullivan a report on what happened. I have a few questions I'd like to ask about your ex-husband, but they can wait. I'll come by your house where we can have some privacy."

"I'm home alone every night after work. Would you give me a call before you stop in?"

Kara went upstairs to look once more at the murder scene. The tape had been taken down and the floor washed. The dressing room mirror had been removed. The wire bin had been stashed under the counter, the items had yet to be reshelved. Everything else seemed the same. She shot a few photos and then went downstairs and out the front door, walking around the building to make sure the man was not lurking, waiting for her to leave.

She got into her car and sat for a few moments. Pulling out her cell phone, she looked down at the picture she'd taken when he'd turned around. It was the face of an angry man, his thin upper lip curled in a stiff sneer. Kara was certain he would not be easily deterred from getting what he wanted. She'd make sure a squad car was assigned to the neighborhood to stay close at hand.

When Kara arrived at the public safety complex, Leo informed her Detective Sullivan was in his office interviewing Superintendent Harknettal and asked if she wanted him to inform Sullivan she was in the building.

"That's okay, Leo. I won't interrupt. He'll fill me in when he calls tonight. I just need to write up an incident report."

Leo handed her a form and when she'd completed it, she asked if he could tell Sergeant Shwinnard she'd like a few minutes of his time. Shwinnard came out and shook her hand. "Hello, Lieutenant! Are you here to stay?"

"No, I'm still a consultant, but I need you to do me a favor." She explained what had happened at Kenyon's, handing him the report. "Make sure we have a police car patrolling the area for the next few days in case this guy decides to return." She sent Shwinnard the picture from her cell.

"Will do. I'll pass on the information to Detective Sullivan. I haven't had a chance to meet with him today. I had some interviews to finish and just arrived, myself. He'll be sorry to have missed you."

"I've got that gift certificate to the Mews. Let's find time to do lunch this week."

Three boxes were set up in front of them as Suzanne and Evelyn went through the garbage bags filled with Sherman's belongings. Vida had packed up two more bags in addition to the ones on her porch. Most of his stuff was ending up in the box marked DUMP. A few things were destined for the recycling bin as soon as Suzanne had run them through the wash.

"He really didn't have much of value," Evelyn said looking at the few items nestled in the bottom of the box marked KEEP.

"He had you and you are definitely a keeper," Suzanne said giving her a hug.

The young woman rested her head on the older woman's shoulder. "I wish I could be sad that he's gone. But I'm not. I don't feel anything. It's wrong to feel nothing when a parent dies."

"Evie, he wasn't much of a parent to you."

"When my mom died, I remember crying myself to sleep every night. Sometimes I still find myself waking up in the middle of a dream about her and wishing I'd stayed asleep. Not wanting to let go. I don't think I'll ever feel like that about him. I have no good memories." She picked up a school yearbook and turned to the page with administrators' photos. His face stared out at her.

"I'm trying to find some happy memories, but I can't. Look at this picture - the way his bottom lip curls down. Always sneering, never a smile. That's how I remember him." She tossed the yearbook into the dump box, but Suzanne took it out and put it with a pile of books and folders at her feet.

"I'll get these back to the school. The principal will probably be at the funeral. I can give them to her there. Let's take a break and I'll make us a nice cup of cocoa."

Kara stood surrounded by teenagers in the school cafeteria. "Lots of hormones loose in this room!" Rosa commented as the two friends stood munching on hot dogs. "Sorry I don't have much to offer you for lunch. Are you sure you don't want a Sloppy Joe?"

"No, three hotdogs are plenty. And this is actually fun. Usually, when I'm at work, I order take-out and sit at my desk doing paperwork during lunch. I like all of the activity. It's electric."

"Exactly! This is one of my favorite times of the day. Do you know, I once had a guidance counselor, a prim, well-dressed woman, tell me she didn't want to be assigned cafeteria duty because her clothes were expensive and she was afraid of a food fight. You'd think she'd want to know what was going on with the kids. This is where I always find out about a potential problem. I can't tell you how many times I've called home to give parents a heads-up about a weekend party being planned at their house while they're away."

"Looks like we have some similarities in our jobs. Keeping your ear to the ground. Better to be proactive than reactive," Kara remarked.

"Amen!" Rosa chuckled as she called a student over to speak with him.

Out in the hallway, Kara saw a figure she recognized walk by. She strode to the doorway. Rosa came up to her and looked in the direction of the figure.

"Who's that?" Kara asked unable to take her eyes off the man who suddenly began to skip.

"Superintendent Harknettal. He must be on his way to the teachers' lounge. He sometimes has lunch with Mr. Porthull – the union rep you interviewed yesterday. They're good buddies. Tight as thieves. Do you want me to introduce you to him?"

"Actually, I met Mr. Harknettal this morning." She showed her friend the photo on her cell that she'd taken of the angry man in Kenyon's.

"What, in heaven's name, is wrong with his face? It looks like he's chewing a mouthful of insects."

"Let's just say he wasn't happy to see me," Kara said.

Back in the principal's office, Kara asked Rosa about her boss. She didn't want to meet him until she'd spoken with Sullivan about their interview that morning. She was glad, now, that she hadn't interrupted them in his office. She thought a second session with her and Sullivan could end up being very interesting.

"I try not to spend much time with the man but I can give you my observations about him as a superintendent. What would you like to know?"

"How long has he been in this district?"

"He was hired four years ago. We'd had a situation with our previous superintendent, Jock Barrette. The female assistant superintendent accused him of harassing her. She hadn't been here for long and was attractive and unfortunately, quite an opportunist. The school committee did not take her seriously, so she went about gathering damning information on him with photos and recordings. Even though they would never have been admitted into a court of law, because Barrett wasn't aware he was being recorded, the school committee quietly paid her off and sent her on her way. Then they worked out a deal with another district to hire Jock as a principal, so they didn't have to fire him. It was a demotion, but at least he had a job and his retirement wasn't in jeopardy."

"Sounds like something from a TV reality show."

"The powers that be hushed it up. The school committee couldn't let the taxpayers know they'd used $200,000.00 in school funds to cover for Jock's indiscretions. This is a small district with limited funds. We had no superintendent and no assistant, so they put an ad in the paper for a new superintendent and a few people applied. You get what you pay for and they ended up with Harknettal."

"I take it you're not impressed with his superintendent skills?"

"He's out of his comfort zone and unfortunately, I make him even more uncomfortable. Whenever he comes into my office to discuss some matter that's been brought to his attention, he ends up frustrated – red-faced and stuttering. He simply doesn't understand what it takes to run a safe school."

"What experience did he have before getting this job?"

"He was a speech counselor and then a special education director in a small town."

"A speech counselor? And he's never run a school district, before?" Kara was amazed.

"He holds a superintendent certificate but he'd never even been a classroom teacher nor was he ever a principal. He's constantly coming in to me regarding some parent who's called complaining about my unfairness to their child."

"You don't strike me as someone who would play favorites."

"You can't do that in this job. Everyone has to be treated equally, or the kids won't trust you. And trust is something you must have to run a safe school."

"Seems like it should be a priority," Kara said.

"I've tried to explain this to Harknettal, but he doesn't agree. He places his popularity ahead of safety. Just recently he came to me with a complaint from a mother because I told her son he couldn't bring his rifle on to school property. She was adamant I change the regulation. Her boy went hunting every afternoon and it was inconvenient for him to go home for the weapon."

"I guess Harknettal didn't know about the zero tolerance policy regarding weapons around schools," Kara said.

"The student displayed the gun in plain view on a rack in the window of his pick-up truck which he left unlocked in the school parking lot."

"You could have had him arrested."

"Harknettal doesn't seem to realize why we aren't acquiescing to every parental demand. I consider him a danger to the safety of the school. He never supports me and I try to do my job with as little communication between us as possible."

"This doesn't seem like a healthy place for you to work."

"It wasn't that bad until three years ago when the school committee decided to hire an assistant principal to take care of discipline, oversee the bookeeping and school supplies."

"And Sherman Pruitt came on the scene."

"He was an old buddy of Harknettal's and came cheap. Harknettal tried to get more money for Pruitt last year by telling me I wasn't getting a pay raise because the school committee didn't like the job I was doing. He'd been writing my evaluations, so I could understand why they might think that way. But I went to them myself and asked what advice they might have for me to improve my performance. They were shocked. The head of the committee commended me on doing a great job. Our test scores were up, dropout levels almost at zero, attendance excellent. I've never had a union grievance filed against me. The committee chair even thanked me profusely for doing more than one job for the past two years and saving them money. They didn't know what I was talking about and assured me the superintendent would be giving me a raise. Harknettal was infuriated. He'd been caught in a lie and I'd gone over his head to speak with them. He threatened to see me fired. I'm sure he'd wanted Pruitt in the job. In some places it's still an 'Ole Boys Club' as far as school administration is concerned."

"I can clearly see that. How do you manage to function in this environment? You don't even have a union."

"True, administrators serve at the whim of the superintendent. Being one of the few female secondary principals in the state, it's important I succeed. I'm not sure what Harknettal has up his sleeve to get rid of me, but with Pruitt out of the way, I'm safe for a while."

"Why do you even want to stay here?"

"In spite of the impression you probably have from some of the staff you've interviewed, most of the teachers here are extremely dedicated. And the kids are great. They deserve better than what they've been saddled with. I'll stay until I'm forced out. And I have a good reputation, so I'm sure I can get another position in a town paying a lot more money, if it comes to that."

There was a knock on the door. It was Sandra informing Principal Brooks that Superintendent Harknettal was in the office waiting to speak with her.

"Tell him I'll be right out. He can walk the corridors with me while I check the lavs for smokers." Rosa raised her right eyebrow and glanced at Kara. "Are you sure you don't want to give me the pleasure of introducing you?"

"No, I think I'll save it for a later date. I'll wait here and leave when he's not around." Kara reached into her purse and brought out Jolene's gift. "For the Giving Tree."

"Thank you. I'll make sure this is delivered. And I'll see you at the board meeting next week. You can tell me all about your interview with my esteemed colleague." Rosa gave her a hug.

Outside, Kara sent Sullivan a text, "We need to meet ASAP."

Sullivan and Shwinnard decided it was a good time to cash in on Kara's offer for lunch. She found them waiting for her at the Mews. They were studying the menu intently when the waiter escorted her to the booth. Sullivan looked up as she skootched in next to him.

"How much is that gift card for? We're both thinking of ordering the most expensive bottle of wine to go along with our lobstas." He used the Rhode Islander's pronunciation.

"Order whatever you want. Lunch is totally on me. I've got a $200.00 gift card but I'm pretty sure they don't serve lobster for lunch and I know you two never drink on the job, so my wallet is safe."

After they'd placed their orders, both men waited for her to speak.

"I'm guessing you both want to know why I summoned you here today?"

Both men chuckled.

"You're guessing right," Shwinnard informed her. "We figure it must be important if you couldn't wait until I called tonight."

Kara brought out her cell phone and passed it to Shwinnard who nodded at the photo and gave it to Sullivan.

"Recognize that handsome face?"

"Superintendent Harknettal. I interrogated him this morning in my office." Sullivan returned the cell to her.

Shwinnard commented, "That's the picture you took of the guy at the store."

"What store?" Sullivan looked at both of them.

"I was at Kenyon's this morning. I wanted to ask Beatrice some questions about her ex. I didn't get the chance. When I arrived, Harknettal was in her office demanding she give him information he wanted. I didn't know who he was at the time and she didn't seem to know him either."

Kara continued her story over lunch and went on to tell them how she'd found out Harknettal was Pruitt's boss.

"That's quite a discovery you've made. He was adamant that I was wasting his time asking him questions. He said he had little to do with Pruitt. I can't wait to interview him again with you in the room."

"I'd like to talk with Beatrice before you bring him in. There has to be a connection in this somewhere," Kara said.

After lunch, they ordered three desserts which were placed at the center of the table to share. Sullivan and Shwinnard spent the rest of the time talking about plans for December and the hope they'd have this case solved so they could enjoy some holiday time with their families. Kara chuckled as they dug into the slices of cake and pies in front of them. She suddenly realized how much she'd enjoyed working with them every day. The gift card was really only for $20.00 but this meal was worth thousands to her.

Wednesday, November 29

6

HERE WE COME A-WASSAILING

"Sophia, what's dis song about?" Gino brought her the sheet music they'd all been given to practice the carols for the town's annual tree lighting ceremony.

His wife began to sing the first few lines of the lyrics he held up in front of her. "Here we come a wassailing among the leaves so green ... "

"Yeah, yeah, yeah. I know da song, but what does it mean? I don't wanna sound stupit if somebody asks me about dis wassail thing."

"The words come from an old Anglo-Saxon greeting meaning 'Be in good health'. It's what people wished each other at Yuletide when the peasants would visit the lord of the manor asking for food and drink. In return for these gifts, the peasants would wish him and his family blessings and goodwill." She sang the last verse of the song, "And God bless you and send you a happy new year, and God send you a happy new year."

"Dat's real nice, Sophia."

"There's actually a drink called wassail and it's mixed in a bowl to share. I think I have my grandmother's recipe somewhere. Would you like me to make up a bowl?"

"Does it have liquor in it?"

"One of the ingredients is mulled wine, from what I remember. My mother made it for a party one year."

"If it's got liquor in it, I'm game. Now, what about dis figgy puddin song ... ?"

"Rick, what time are we supposed to be at the Tavern Hall Club? I deleted the email Clay sent," Ruth called out the door to her fiancé. Snow had been falling all afternoon and he was outside shoveling a path down the walkway.

He stopped for a minute to check his iPhone. "Rehearsal starts at 7 o'clock."

"I told Arthur we'd collect him early and take him to Sa-Tang for Thai food. He called to say he's starved. Are we supposed to pick up Sophia and Gino?"

"No, I just talked to my brother and they're running late. Sophia is making some kind of drink to bring and he was rushing around looking for ingredients. He called to see if we had any mulled ale or curdled cream."

"Wassail?" Ruth called out.

"Wassup with you?" Rick called back.

"No, the drink. It's wassail. Do they need a pewter bowl? I have one."

"You'll have to call her yourself. If this snow doesn't stop soon, I could be shoveling all night long."

"Kara, come join me for a spot of tea," Stewart kissed his wife and helped her off with her coat.

"Don't mind if I do," she said. "What's this?"

"A figgy pudding, my dear."

"Figgy pudding? Like in the song?" She wasn't sure what to expect from the dish resting on the top of their stove."

"Now bring us a figgy pudding, now bring us a figgy pudding, now bring us a figgy pudding and a cup of good cheer." Stewart had a wonderful voice and he decided to sing the lyrics in what he believed was his finest English accent. Kara was worried this might be the start of a long night. Stewart enjoyed mimicking different accents but cockney was not one of his best.

"Come eeyah, moy deeyah and take a strong wiff a this odiferous con-coct-ion!" He led her by the hand to his masterpiece. The aroma filled the kitchen with hints of dried fruit and nuts and brandy. And it was a healthy shade of brown, not green! That meant no avocados or pesto or asparagus were used in the making of this dessert! Kara silently rejoiced.

"It smells intoxicating, Stewart."

"You look gobsmacked, my dear." He offered her a spoonful.

"I really believe this is one of your best endeavors."

"By George, I think I've got it! My very first figgy pudding!"

She gave him another kiss. "I'm going to take a quick shower before we go out."

"I'll bring your cuppa up to you, Madam." He bowed.

"Kara wasn't sure whether to curtsy or run from the room.

"Pip, pip, cheerio. On yer way, ma luv!" He said patting her on the butt.

She could only hope he intended to pour a gallon of brandy on that pudding.

"Jess, what time can I put him to bed?" Carl Sullivan had just given his two year old a bath and was now trying to chase down the little guy who was running around the house naked.

"Oh, he got into the candy canes again and he has a lot of sugar in his system. Maybe you should just let him run it off," his wife advised.

"What time do you think you'll be home?" He was reaching under the table trying to grab hold of the boy who was using the puppy as a shield between him and his father.

"Probably after ten. Rehearsal could last at least two hours and then we need to get our costumes."

"Isn't that kind of late for Billy to be out on a school night?"

"They need some younger kids for the carolers and he has the best soprano voice in the chorus. His music teacher is giving the students who participate extra credit and they have permission to come into school late tomorrow."

Her husband had managed to grab the dog and pull it out into the open, but Connor was too smart to fall for that ploy. He stayed safely under the table, yanking at the cloth to hide himself from view.

Utensils fell on the floor and then a melamine dish full of spaghetti, meatballs and tomato sauce spilled upside-down on Max's head.

"Bus-geddy hat!" The little boy crowed as the pup began to use his paws to wipe the meal from his fur on to the floor, noisily lapping it all up.

"Maybe the committee could use a Victorian baby? We could find an old English pram to put him in and you could bring him with you tonight. He'd look adorable in a little white laced bonnet." At this moment, Carl felt his youngest son would look adorable in anything since he couldn't seem to hold him long enough to get a diaper on him. This was going to be a very long night.

Beatrice left the office later than she expected. She'd remained open for some last-minute shoppers. She sent the clerks home and finished ringing up the sales herself.

A police cruiser went by the front of the store and stopped. She'd noticed the police keeping watch on her during the day and it made her feel safer. As she went through the basement and the first floor, emptying cash registers and turning off lights, the sound of floorboards creaked overhead.

She walked up the wide staircase and onto the second landing cautiously, looking expectantly over at the dressing room where Sherman's body had lain only a few days ago. The curtain was open and the cracked mirror had been replaced. A faint light from the street lamp outside filled the back of the room causing shadows to move along the walls.

Beatrice was relieved when she returned to her office and put the day's cash into the safe and locked up the file cabinet. She made a final check of the front and side doors to make sure they were locked. The last thing she did was to turn off the music that had been playing throughout the store all day long. She waited until the familiar Old English tune about caroling among the leaves so green finished. It was one of her favorites.

Exiting into the parking lot, she sighed. The car was covered in snow and she hadn't brought a brush with her, but she didn't have far to drive and the wipers would take care of clearing the windshield.

She wished for one of those remote starters to warm up her car before coming out into the frosty air. The door was frozen shut and Bea yanked hard, then took a minute to check the back seat, making sure no one was hiding.

Her breath came out in steamy bursts as she turned on the ignition and pumped the gas pedal. The engine failed to start. She tried it a few more times causing the vehicle to flood. A strong smell of gasoline filled the air as she took out her cell to call Ed to see if he could give her a jump-start. But her phone was almost dead. As usual, she'd neglected to recharge it. Rather than go back into the store, she decided to take the short walk to her house. From the parking lot she glanced up to see if the lights on her Christmas tree were lit. They were on an automatic timer. The house was still in darkness.

Beatrice got out of the car and looked around. Members of the Wakefield Village Association were out on Main Street putting up Christmas decorations in preparation for the traditional tree lighting on Saturday night. She waved to her neighbors as they hung a bright green wreath with shiny, red, holly berries on the lamp post at the corner. She thought again about going back inside to call but instead she turned and left the lot.

A figure slouched in the doorway arch of the church across the street. He slid out of the shadows watching her trudge up the hill toward the house. The tree and the candles in her front window suddenly burst into light as she moved slowly toward home unaware she was being followed.

"Evelyn, are you sure I can't make you some dinner before I leave?"

"No thanks, Suzy," she was comfortably ensconced on the couch with a quilt and a pillow watching the 1951 black and white version of *A Christmas Carol* starring Alastair Sims. "I'll be fine. If I get hungry, I'll just eat cookies. What time is Buddy supposed to be in?"

"He and some of his friends are setting up the outdoor crèche at the Baptist church. They'll probably walk up to the Wakefield Mall when they're done and get something to eat. I don't think he'll be home any later than eleven. Don't worry about him. Everybody's out tonight decorating the sidewalks for the weekend festivities."

"Oh, I love this scene!"

Suzy was putting on her coat but came in from the hallway to watch as Mrs. Crotchet lit the whiskey soaked plum pudding and her husband tasted it with much ceremony. The family waited in breathless anticipation until their father gave his hearty approval of the desert he'd been served.

"One little cake to divide among so many mouths and they were still happy." Suzy pulled a red toque over her ears and plucked green mittens from her pocket. "It's starting to snow again. I wouldn't mind staying home tonight and watching old Christmas movies. Did you find *It's a Wonderful Life?*"

Evelyn patted the pile of DVDs next to her on the end table. "That's next on the list."

"Have fun and I shouldn't be home too late, either. Maybe we'll stay up and do a Christmas movie marathon?"

"I promise I won't watch *Scrooged* without you," Evelyn called to her as she turned out the light to enjoy the rest of Dickens' classic in the dark.

Members of the Kingston Improvement Association were trying to organize the costumes and find clothes to fit each of the singers. Since their village didn't have an official tree lighting, they were putting all of their energies into the celebrations in downtown Wakefield. More than enough people had shown up for the caroling. They'd been separated into two groups to wander at opposite ends of Main Street, stopping at local businesses and homes to perform.

It had soon become evident to the musical director, during the rehearsal, that not all of the volunteers could hold a tune. Clay Van Zinck was not easily daunted. He'd produced all manner of music festivals and concerts and was well-prepared for this minor problem.

He handed his list of wannnabe singers to his assistants who informed the rejected singers they'd been chosen to play the part of elves and pass out candy canes to the younger children who'd come with their parents to see Santa.

"Sophia, Ruth, look!" They turned to find Gino holding a Santa outfit in front of him. "I get ta be the big honcho! Ho! Ho! Ho!" He held his stomach and roared out, "Merry Christmas! Hohoho!"

"I can't think of anyone else who could do it better, Darling." Making sure he didn't look toward the wardrobe closet where a woman was distributing another Santa outfit to their friend, Arthur, Sophia distracted her husband by calling his attention to the bag of candy canes and trinkets he'd been given along with the outfit.

"The children will love you. You'll be the best Saint Nick ever in the history of South County," Ruth said.

"I never got asked ta be Santa before," he confided in his friends. His eyes welled up with grateful tears.

"Grab the punch bowl. We need to leave. I've got an early shift at the hospital tomorrow. Say 'So long' to everybody." He managed to give a quick wave before Sophia had steered him out the door.

Arthur joined the group wearing his Santa beard and hat. "Look, they asked me to play Santa! How great is that?"

"Congratulations, Arthur," Kara said.

"Hey, Gino has the same …" Ruth stuck her elbow into Rick's chest before he could finish the sentence.

"Are we all ready to go?" she asked, shooting her fiancé a warning look

"Can we stop and get something to eat?"

"Arthur, it's late. You had appetizers and a full meal at the Thai restaurant just a few hours ago!"

"But we didn't have time for dessert and I'm still hungry."

"When are you not hungry?" Ruth laughed as her old friend tried to look pathetic. "Okay, where would you like to go?"

"Mary Murphy's." He rushed toward the exit.

"The man is a bottomless pit," Rick declared.

"Kara!" Jess Sullivan called to her. "Carl just phoned to see when I'd be home. He asked me to give you a message. Beatrice Pruitt has disappeared."

"Thanks, Jess, I'll call him right now." She caught up with the others in the parking lot. "Stewart, why don't you go with Ruth and Rick? I'm going to take our car and meet up with Carl."

"Do you want me to keep you company?" he asked.

"No, I just need to check on something. I shouldn't be late."

"Call when you start for home and I'll have some tea ready for you."

Her friends waved as she stood watching them leave. She phoned Carl Sullivan and could hear a child screeching in the background.

"The station called a few minutes ago. Ed Tucker stopped in to report Beatrice Pruitt's car is still in the lot at Kenyon's. She'd left a message on his phone at around six asking him to stop by after he finished his shift. She said her car wouldn't start again and she'd walked home. He went by the house and the door was unlocked, but she wasn't there. I told him I'd be by as soon as my wife got home."

"She's on her way, now. I'll drive over and see if there's anything I can do."

"Connor, put that down. Max get off the couch! Sorry, Kara. I have to go. I'll meet you at Beatrice's. And thanks," he said as the sound of something crashing followed by a child's screams and a dog barking brought the phone call to an abrupt end.

7

Brightly Shone the Moon That Night, Though the Frost Was Cruel

Ed Tucker was standing at the front door when Kara arrived. She noted that the Christmas tree and the lights in the window were on. As she walked up the front path, Sullivan's car pulled into the driveway.

Tucker let them into the house. "Thanks for coming by. I know you need to wait twenty-four hours before filing a missing person's report, but I'm really worried. Bea doesn't usually go out at night and her car is in the lot at the store, covered in snow. With the murder and all, I didn't want to wait."

"You did the right thing," Sullivan told him. "Let's see if we can sort this out. What time did she leave the message?"

He took out his phone. "Quarter past six – I guess when she got out of work. I didn't see it until I checked my texts at 8:45, just before I finished my shift. The kids are staying at a neighbor's, so I headed over to the store to see if the car was still there. It was, and I came here. The door was open and the Christmas lights were on. They're on a timer. But Bea wasn't here. Her cell phone's in the kitchen."

"Is there anywhere else she could be?" Kara asked.

"I phoned her sister-in-law, Suzanne, and she said she hadn't seen her since Friday night when she stopped by to tell her about Sherman."

"What about friends?"

"Bea keeps to herself. She has some acquaintances, but no real friends."

"Have you spoken with any of her neighbors?" Sullivan noticed the lights on in adjacent houses. Across the street was a stone wall in front of a wooded lot.

"No, I checked around the house and then called you right away. I had your card in my pocket." He took out the card to show them.

"I'll go next door and see if they can give me some information. Detective Langley will stay here with you."

When Sullivan left, Kara walked around the inside of the house. Tucker followed close behind.

"Is anything out of place?" Kara asked him.

"Bea is a minimalist. She doesn't keep much stuff around and nothing seems to be disturbed," he informed her.

In the kitchen Kara found a pocketbook which she opened to examine the contents: Kleenex; a change purse filled with coins; a wallet with a few small bills inside; a set of keys; a package of Fisherman's Friend cough drops. Beatrice's cell phone was charging on the counter. The last call made was to Tucker She looked through the contacts. "Do you know any of these people?"

They scanned the short alphabetical list and he recognized most of the names. She noticed that Vida Koranski was on the list although Sherman wasn't.

"Does Beatrice know Vida well?"

"They met at an Alcoholics Anonymous meeting. I think Vida was her sponsor," Ed said.

She wondered if Sullivan was aware of this. "Does Beatrice go to many meetings?"

"Not lately. Bea says she's taken care of the problem and doesn't need the program."

"Do you think the problem's solved?"

"I'm worried. Bea told me she's been having blackouts lately and can't remember whole periods of time."

"Has this happened often to your knowledge?"

"I'm not sure. Once I found her roaming around the neighborhood and I drove her home. She didn't remember any of it when we met again. I never spent that much time with her before last year

84

although we've been friends a long time. Since my wife left, we've been helping each other. She's real good with the kids. But I can't say that she ever confides in me. So, I don't know for sure."

Kara had been checking the kitchen cupboards and moved to the side so Tucker could see the liquor bottle inside the cabinet under the sink. He just looked at her, shook his head and went to sit on the couch in the living room.

The bedroom was quite stark, holding few of the feminine touches she would have expected. But propped against the pillow at the top of the bed was a doll, its delicate China blue laced dress fanned out around it. A frilled parasol with a thin shaft was clutched in the pale hand and rested above a head of golden banana curls. In the top drawer of the bureau, Kara found a listing of AA meetings with places and times. She heard Sullivan's voice calling the station to make a report and ask to have police sent to search the woods across the street. She signaled him to go outside with her so they could talk in private.

"I found a list of AA meetings and it looks like there was one at the Baptist Church down the street tonight at eight. If no one picked her up and if she left here on foot, she has to be close by. Did you know Vida Koranski was once her sponsor?"

"Vida told me Beatrice went to meetings but she never mentioned she was her sponsor. I'll call her and ask her why she left that out in our little talk," Sullivan said.

"She may have been afraid you'd ask questions she considered confidential information," Kara suggested.

Two patrol cars arrived and Sullivan informed them of Bea's disappearance. They took searchlights to begin a sweep of the woods. The moon had come out from behind the clouds and the frigid air had turned the soft snowfall of the early evening hours into a thick, icy coating, which, in the stillness, crunched under their feet.

"I'm going to take a walk over to the church and see if I can find anyone still there."

"I'll walk to Main Street with you. Suzanne Tetreault's expecting me. She says Beatrice hasn't been in touch in the last few days, but

I'm going to go to the apartment to see for myself," Sullivan said. He told the officers he'd be returning and to call if they needed him.

They went down the hill in silence, stopping in the store lot to open Bea's car. Carl popped open the trunk and inside they found only jumper cables, and a tire jack. Her car was as neat as the inside of her house and just as sparse. The back door of the department store was locked.

"I'll call you if I find out anything," Kara said as she watched him cross the deserted street in front of Kenyon's.

As Kara moved along the shoveled sidewalks on her way to the church, it was beginning to get colder and she put her hands into her pockets. She passed by Brickleys' Ice Cream, now closed for the season and remembered the warm summers of her youth. On weekdays, she would run along these sidewalks to bring her father his lunch pail filled with fresh baked bread, ham and cheese sandwiches and a big, warm slice of apple or peach pie her mom had baked. Her dad had worked for years at the Wakefield Branch. She loved sitting outside the lumber yard listening to him and other workers trade stories about when the tracks of the Narragansett Pier Railroad once brought trains into the village making it a bustling manufacturing center.

She still could hear his voice in her head. "Did you know, Kara, that in 1765 you could take take a boat on the Saugatucket River into the village? There was a tavern, a stagecoach stop and a snuff mill." (She would always ask him to tell her about the snuff mill.) "Later, when the train tracks were layed, there was a grist mill, a saw mill, and a blacksmith shop," he said pointing in the direction where those buildings once stood. She knew from his stories, that her great grandfather had been the blacksmith – "He was a vital member of the community," her father never forgot to remind her. "It's important we all do our jobs and make our community safe and prosperous." Kara remembered how proud he'd been when she was sworn in as a police officer.

She crossed over the bike path where the tracks once had been and looked toward the Wakefield Baptist Church, built in 1830 for the families beginning to settle in the town. Kara walked past the life-sized crèche on the front lawn and up the back steps leading into the church hall.

The tree in Suzanne's apartment was still lit. A slight movement at the kitchen window caught his eye. A hand on the top of the candle on the sill twisted the bulb, casting the window and the room behind it into darkness.

He was met at the second floor landing by Suzanne who ushered him into the warm living room where she told him to make himself comfortable.

"Do you have any news of my sister-in-law?" She sat down heavily in the chair nearest the Christmas tree.

"Ed Tucker reported her missing over an hour ago and we've been trying to get some leads on where she might be."

"Ed is very level-headed. He wouldn't have called if he thought Bea wasn't in some kind of trouble. He's known her since childhood."

"We have a team of officers searching the woods across from her house. I've spoken with the neighbors and one of them said she waved to them earlier in the evening. They were helping decorate the town for the tree lighting festivities this weekend."

"You mentioned when you phoned that her car was still at the store across the street. She told me last week she'd been having trouble with it starting."

"She'd left a message with Ed and he drove to the lot after work. He went to her house after stopping to check the car and that's when he found she wasn't at home," Sullivan said.

Evelyn came into the room with a tray of cookies and hot chocolate and placed it on the end table. She handed him a mug and offered him a napkin and a plate.

"Thanks. How're you doing?"

"I'm still trying to get things straightened out. My father didn't leave much and I'm afraid there'll be bills to pay in the coming weeks. Suzy's been helping me go through his papers and sort out what we can." She nodded her head to the boxes stacked in the corner of the room.

"I'd like to look over those papers to see if anything could help us find his killer."

"You're welcome to it all. Anything in that carton is going to be tossed out and there's another box of stuff to be recycled," Evelyn said. He rose to take the box from the top of the pile and they began helping him go through some of the things inside.

Lights were on in the church hall. People were milling around drinking coffee. Some were folding chairs and storing them away in the closets under the stage. As Kara was looking to see if Beatrice was in the room, an older woman came to ask if she could be of help.

"I was wondering if Beatrice Pruitt had left yet," she asked.

"I'm relatively new here. I don't recognize that name, but maybe someone else will know? My name's Corinne. I'll ask around for you. Would you like a cup of coffee?"

"I'm Kara. No, thanks, I haven't been drinking much coffee lately."

"I'll get you some hot water and I'm sure we've got tea bags somewhere in the kitchen."

"I'd appreciate a warm drink. It seemed much milder earlier in the evening and now I'm wishing I'd brought my gloves," she said as the woman handed her a cup. Kara stood in the kitchen sipping the steaming liquid, watching people filter out of the building.

Corrine returned with a younger woman. "Kara, this is Deidre. She recognized the name Pruitt."

"Yes, a guy named Pruitt sat next to me at a meeting about a month ago. I don't remember his first name, but I felt he wasn't really there to get help. He gave me the impression he was trying to get a date. I let him know I wasn't interested."

"Sherman Pruitt?" Kara offered.

"Yeah, that was it. Sherman. Creepy guy. And I could smell liquor on his breath. I was sitting in the back row, but moved up front away from him. I haven't seen him at any meetings since."

Kara thanked the two women and drank her tea as they went to finish cleaning up. She waited until the lights were switched off to step outside.

The parking lot soon emptied out and the night turned to darkness as cloud cover sheathed the moon. A brisk wind swiftly moved it along as it passed over clusters of stars and she searched for the star the Magi had followed in their journey to find the newborn king. She wondered if the Baby Jesus had been placed into the Nativity scene out front. Sometimes, she'd been told, the baby would not be brought to the manger until Chrisms Eve.

All of the ceramic figures were in attendance. Mary and Joseph, the shepherds and their sheep, the wise men and their camels. An angel perched atop the structure, standing watch over the human figures who were settled in among the straw and the animals. She went up to the crèche and found the babe in swaddling clothes sleeping peacefully in his manger. She whispered a short prayer.

They'd just opened the second box when the teenager Sullivan had collided with on his first visit to the apartment entered the room. He stood stiffly next to the couch appearing to be waiting for some instruction.

"This is my nephew, Buddy. Buddy, this is Detective Sullivan. He's working on your step-father's case."

Sullivan stood up and stretched out his hand, which the boy grasped in a firm shake. "I can help you put these boxes in your police car if you'd like," he said.

"Thanks, I appreciate the offer, but my car is still up the road at your mother's." He explained to Suzanne, "Detective Langley and I walked from there."

"You should give her a call and ask if she'd like to come up and get warm. The temperature has really dropped since this afternoon."

"She's down the street at the Baptist church. There's an AA meeting tonight. She wanted to see if Mrs. Pruitt could have gone there from the house."

The two women gave each other a side-glance but said nothing.

"I was at the church earlier," the boy said. "Some of my friends and I helped set up the outside Nativity display. There were lots of people on the sidewalks, but I didn't see my mom."

"The snow has been trampled and trying to detect one set of footprints would be impossible. It looks like quite a few people are getting ready for Saturday's celebration," Sullivan said. "Do you know if your sister-in-law still attends meetings?" He threw out the question to all of them but before they could answer, his cell phone rang.

He looked at the caller ID and it was Kara. "I'll just be a minute," he explained as he stepped into the hall and closed the door.

From the rear of the tableau, something had shifted ever so slightly. Kara ducked her head and went in, moving Joseph to one side. Using her cell phone to light the creche, she detected movement next to a white lamb in sore need of a fresh coat of paint. An orange glove appeared. She thought she heard a weak moan. Kara dropped to her knees, digging away at the straw. She felt for a pulse then dialed 911 to call for an ambulance. The sound of sirens soon pierced the cold night air. She pushed another button on the phone. "Carl, I'm still at the church. I've found Beatrice Pruitt."

Thursday, November 30

8

BLUE, BLUE, BLUE HOLIDAY

On Thursday morning, Sophia called from the hospital to give Kara an update on Beatrice's condition. "She's lapsing in and out of consciousness and is very weak. They've placed her on a heart monitor. Her body temperature was extremely low when the ambulance brought her in. She'd be dead if you hadn't started CPR. I'm not sure she's going to make it."

"I'll come by later in the afternoon."

"I hope you've had your flu shot. This place is filled to capacity with sick people. Beatrice is in a private room. Her friend Ed Tucker came in for a few minutes. We told him to call tomorrow to see if he can visit. Suzanne Tetreault came by. They're limiting visitors to family, but I'll get you in to see her if you're here before my shift ends. Although, I may have to put in overtime."

"Thanks, Sophia. I'll call when I'm done."

Carl Sullivan had phoned to tell her he'd dropped the clothes Beatrice had been wearing off at the lab. They still were not sure if foul play was involved and were treating the area around the crèche as a potential crime scene. Kara would be helping Dr. Hill examine the clothes for evidence, if there was any to be found. "I'm going to have another talk with Hyram Harknettal this afternoon. Would you like to come along as an added surprise?"

"I was planning on speaking with Beatrice first before meeting with him, but that doesn't look very likely at this point. I'll stop by the station. What time were you planning your visit?"

"Let's make it for 2:45 and ruin his day. He likes to leave work early. According to his secretary, he tells her he's going to meetings, but she's friends with a neighbor of his who sees him jogging every day even before the school buses have dropped the kids off."

"Run a check on the last few positions he's held. A resume would be a good place to start although people lie on resumes all the time. I have a funny feeling he might have things to hide and I like to know the answers to my questions before I ask them. It'll be apparent soon into the interview if he's telling the truth," she said.

"I spoke with your friend, Sophia, this morning at the hospital and asked her to keep me updated on Beatrice's condition."

"She's got her hands full on the pediatric ward but she'll look in on Beatrice during her break. They did some toxicology tests and I'll be interested in the findings. See you this afternoon."

Dr. Hill was in the lab when she arrived. "I have to test fire this .38 but I'll be with you in a few minutes." He took a pair of ear plugs from the box on the counter and went into the next room. Kara began to lay out Beatrice's clothes for examination.

The soles of the boots would be scraped and residue tested in hopes something in the tread could help in tracking her movements. The heavily insulated down jacket, which reminded Kara of the Pillsbury Doughboy, probably helped save the woman's life. Thick woolen socks, mittens and scarf were set aside to be examined for hairs or fibers. She hadn't detected blood or stains on either the outer clothing or the slacks and sweater, but they would be placed under a scan and traces removed to be tested. As she looked at the clothes laid out in front of her, something nudged in her mind. Something was not right. The gloves. She was distracted by Hill's return.

"I missed you at Friday's talk on incendiary devices. Not something you deal with every day, but interesting in how a bomb squad processes a crime scene. It can be pretty messy," he wrinkled his nose.

"I'll have to catch that lecture on video."

Hill took a CD from the shelf and slipped the disc into his player. He began to strum an air guitar, doing his best impression of Elvis performing "Blue Christmas". Kara grabbed a pair of plugs from the box and with great ceremony, inserted them into her ears.

Rick stopped by the Courthouse Center for the Arts where his brother worked. Gino told him he'd be on the second floor setting up for the crafts fair scheduled for the weekend. When his brother arrived, the tables were in place and the large room looked festive. Christmas trees with flashing blue and white fairy lights were in every corner. Star lights were suspended from a navy blue background hung from the ceiling. On a platform, a family of seals was building a gigantic snowman surrounded by a grove of paper birch trees, their branches encased in strings of silver twinkling lights.

"Wow! The place looks great, Gino. I feel like I've been transported to an ice castle. How long have you been working on this?"

"Since Tuesday mornin. I wanted to make sure it got done ahead a time. Ya like it?"

Gino felt Rick was the true artist in the family and he valued his brother's opinion, especially when it came to anything having to do with art. Gino had been a window designer in New York City and he'd always called Rick in to give him advice before he launched anything on the public.

"It's gorgeous. I love the different shades of blue in the sky and the aqua tint in the ice floes."

"Yeah, and we can save on heat cuz we wanna create a cool atmosphere."

"Do you ever miss New York?" His brother sat on a ledge next to a polar bear and her cubs.

"Sometime around the holidays, I do. How 'bout dose bears? I did a thing for Coca Cola once and when the show wuz done, they wuz gonna trow em out. So I took em home wid me. Sophia made me keep em in the garage, but they were the inspiration for dis whole extravaganza."

"I think I could just stay here for the rest of the day," Rick said.

"We can't. I gotta get Sophia her Christmas present and I need you ta help me pick it out."

"I guess we'll be spending time in a few jewelry stores, then?"

"You guessed right. But the good news is we don't have ta look at everything. Only the sapphires. It's gonna be a blue Christmas for Sophia."

"Well, that whittles it down to a few hours. I'll call Ruth and tell her not to expect me for dinner."

Ruth ended the call. She turned to her old friend, Arthur, who was studying the list of books they'd be using for the course they were planning to teach together the following semester. "That was Rick. He and Gino are doing their Christmas shopping this afternoon. He won't be home until later. So, would you be my date for dinner? We could see if any of the old gang is at Meldgies."

"You said the magic words. I've never turned down a meal in all of my years on this earth. And maybe you could take me to the book store afterwards so I can do my Christmas shopping?"

"Sounds like the perfect date to me." She and Arthur enjoyed finding new authors' titles on the mystery shelves at Wakefield Books. They spent hours discussing the character development and plot of some of their favorite writers' works.

It had taken her years to convince Arthur to co-teach a class with her, but now, he was showing enthusiasm about the prospect of sharing his knowledge with her senior honors class. They'd each chosen three modern novels and the final selection for the course would be A Quiet Death. This was the book that had earned Arthur a Pulitzer Prize for Literature back in the 60s when he was a young man beginning his career in New York City.

Today they'd completed the final edits on the syllabus. Ruth had placed orders at the campus book store and they finally could sit back and relax.

"How are the wedding plans coming along?"

"Sophia has it all well in hand. I've tried my best to keep out of her way. You know me, I'm not much for planning anything that involves more than a few close friends sharing a pot-luck dinner."

"Sounds to me like you should have eloped."

"I agree, but Rick is pretty excited about the idea of a Christmas wedding."

"Rick? The quiet guy you're engaged to? The one who hardly says anything?"

"Yup, that's the one. He and Sophia have been meeting on a regular basis to make sure everything is perfect. Then they send Gino off to carry out their plans."

"And you're not the least bit worried about any of this?"

"Nope, as long as I don't have to get involved, whatever they do is fine with me. But there is one thing … I was hoping you'd do a reading at the ceremony. It would mean a lot to me."

"A reading? From anything in particular?"

"No, you choose. I'm sure you'll find the exact right words."

"That reminds me. I have something for you."

He took out a small box and handed it to her. Inside was a blue linen handkerchief, its outer edges crocheted in a delicate creamy lace.

"Why, this is lovely Arthur."

"It was my mother's … from her wedding day. You know … something borrowed, something blue. Her mother made it for her." He brushed his fingers across his eyes. Ruth reached out to him and for the longest time the two old friends sat in comfortable silence, holding hands.

The clock on the wall of the forensics lab made a sharp buzzing sound as the hand moved to the hour. Kara took the note she'd found in Beatrice's coat pocket, put away the scarf and gloves she was examining and patted Dr. Hill on the back. He was hunched over his desk engrossed in filling out a report and humming along with Perry Como's rendition of "White Christmas".

"Hey, where are you off to?"

"I told Detective Sullivan I'd sit in on an interview this afternoon. I've already examined the coat for trace evidence. I'll finish this up tomorrow."

He nodded and returned to the paperwork in front of him.

Kara called to inform Leo she'd be at the safety complex in five minutes.

"Superintendent Harknettal just arrived. Detective Sullivan said to tell you they're in your office and not to knock. Just go right in," he said.

She could hear the superintendent's complaints of undue harassment even before she walked into the room. Sullivan, who was leaning against the wall, nodded toward the desk where he had positioned her name plate in front of the irate man in the chair with his back to her.

"Good afternoon, Lieutenant Langley," Sullivan greeted her.

Harknettal twisted around to see who had entered the room. There was a moment of surprised recognition that turned to barely suppressed rage as it dawned on him where he'd first seen her.

"I don't believe you've been properly introduced. Detective Langley, this is Superintendent Hyram Harknettal." He started to rise and then sat back down. His hands clutched at the arms of the chair, knuckles white. The color drained from his face giving his skin a bluish pallor in the fluorescent lighting of the office.

Understanding Sullivan's motive for wanting her to conduct the interview, Kara moved into the seat behind her old desk. Without acknowledging their previous meeting, she opened the folder in front of her and carefully looked through it, letting this odious man stew for awhile before addressing him.

"Mr. Harknettal, let me convey my condolences on the loss of your friend, Mr. Sherman Pruitt."

"I'd h-h-hardly c-c-cconsider Pruitt my friend. We worked together, th-th-that's all."

"How long have you known him?"

"I t-told you, we worked t-t-together since he was hired to be the assistant principal until he was f-fired last month."

"You didn't know him before then?" She made a point of picking up one of the sheets from the folder in front of her.

"We d-d-d-did work in the same d-d-d-district in Massachusetts. Out on the Cape. He was the janitor at the middle school. I was the special ed director. Our paths never crossed. I had no cause to spend time any time with him."

She held up two sheets of paper, one in each hand, silently comparing them. Harknettal sat ramrod straight in his chair, sensing she had further questions he may not want to answer.

"I noticed on your resume you received a superintendent's certificate. The date on this copy is May of 2007."

"That would be correct. I took a s-s-sabbatical f-from my job to get a d-d-d-degree in administration."

"A sabbatical? How long was that"

"A semester."

"I would imagine there would be quite a few courses to take in order to be certified."

"There was course work involved and I received c-c-credit for my work experience and transfer c-c-credits from the University of RI."

"I can see that. So, after one semester at Louisville, you qualified for your administrative certificate?"

"Yes."

"And it appears Mr. Pruitt received the same certificate in 2008."

"From my understanding, Mr. Pruitt took courses at URI. He received a degree in physical education and got a job here in RI teaching at one of the middle schools."

"And a few years later, he took classes to become certified in school administration. At the University of Louisville?" she asked.

"The administrator in charge of m-m-middle school educators ran a p-program at URI. When he was hired for the job at Louisville, some students followed him. Therefore, Lieutenant, it could easily be a c-c-coincidence."

"So, you worked in the same district as Pruitt on Cape Cod. You both took courses at URI and you both received advanced credits at the University of Louisville toward administrative certification. Yet, socially, your paths never crossed?"

"It's a big world, Lieutenant. His career path was as a janitor, a phys ed teacher and an assistant principal. Mine was as a sp-sp-speech counselor, a p-program director and a superintendent of schools. Sherman and I obviously didn't inhabit the s-s-same s-social strata."

"In your time working as Mr. Pruitt's boss, did you or anyone have issues with him?"

"Not until he ran into p-problems with Brooks. The teachers seemed to like him. He never did anything to get him in t-trouble with the union and he always had his reports in on t-t-time."

"Why did you decide to fire him?"

"I chose not to renew his c-c-contract because of personal issues he was having that interfered with his job. If Brooks hadn't encouraged the young woman to file a c-complaint and we weren't in the m-m-middle of this ridiculous, feminist M-M-Metoo Movement, I'm sure he'd st-still have his job. It isn't easy right now, for men. All these females m-m-making m-m-mountains out of m-m-m-molehills."

Sullivan opened his mouth to say something to Harknettal but a glance from Kara caused him to stay quiet.

"When was the last time you saw Mr. Pruitt?"

"He came to my office the day he was given notice. He asked if there was something I could d-do for him. Obviously, my hands were tied. I d-d-did agree to give him a reference. It's in his permanent file."

"Thank you for coming in, Superintendent."

Harknettal looked relieved and got up to leave.

"Oh, I have one more question for you."

He stiffened and turned back to face her.

"Exactly what was it you were looking for when you went to visit Mrs. Pruitt at the department store yesterday?"

"Sherman left a m-message on my machine that he'd given his ex a folder for me. He said it was thanks for g-g-giving him a good reference. He didn't offer any details. He just said it was in a file cabinet and contained critical information I needed to know."

"Why would he leave it with his ex-wife? He hadn't been in contact with her for months."

"I d-don't know where you're getting your information, D-D-Detective, but he t-t-told me they'd been together for a while. Are you finished?"

She nodded at him and when he turned toward the door, she added, much to Sullivan's delight, "You have my permission to leave."

Sophia had finished her shift and headed to the Intensive Care Unit. As she stepped inside the elevator, a boy moved to the back. He kept his head down under a Yankee's baseball cap and seemed to be avoiding eye contact. When she got off, he remained inside as the elevator began its descent back to the main floor. She stopped at the desk and one of the nurses at the station told her there had been little change in the patient.

The room was dark and after scanning the monitors, Sophia made herself comfortable in a chair in the corner of the room. She'd done two shifts. Exhaustion and the heat inside the room caused her to nod off to sleep, awaking only when Kara arrived an hour later.

"Hey, Sleepyhead." Kara lightly touched her friend's arm.

"Kara. What time is it?"

"A little after four."

"I drowsed off." She looked at Beatrice. A blanket had been placed over the bed sheet.

"That's nice, Kara. Something pretty for her when she wakes up."

Kara saw Bea's thin form lying still under the covers and nestled next to her was the round face of the porcelain doll, its two steely grey eyes staring up to the ceiling. "I didn't bring that in," Kara said.

"Somebody else must have brought it to her while I was sleeping. I saw a boy with a Yankee baseball cap and a backpack when I came up on the elevator."

Walking over to the bed, Kara took the doll out from under the blanket. Its china blue dress flounced over the lacey pantaloons and the parasol fell on to the floor. Sophia picked it up. The golden curls bobbled to and fro and Kara examined it more closely to find that the doll's head had come loose and was being held in place by the tight collar of lace around the neck.

Sophia stepped outside to ask if the staff on duty had noticed anyone entering the room. They assured her they'd seen no one coming or going since she'd arrived. Just at that moment, the heart monitor began to beep loudly. The head nurse called out, "Code Blue" alerting members of the team to rush to Beatrice's room.

The tranquility of the ward had been shattered. Kara was asked to leave and she and Sophia stood in the corridor waiting anxiously while the nurses and doctors worked feverishly to resuscitate their patient.

He took off his baseball cap when he entered and looked up at the stained-glass window. It had always been his favorite. The gentle eyes of St. Francis looked down on him as he waited in the pew for the priest to open the confessional and perform the weekly sacrament of Penance. He'd often dreamt of hiding under those flowing, heavenly blue robes, protected from the myriad of things he feared. If anyone dared to approach, those powerful arms would reach down, battering away at the weak mortals trying to wrench him out into a world fraught with dangers.

He heard the side door open and then quiet footsteps. He watched from the shadows until the priest was safely inside. Kneeling in the dark, confined space, the small window slid opened as he began the prayer he knew so well, "Bless me Father for I have sinned … "

Friday, December 1

9

Dressed in Holiday Style

"Mommy, mommy, mommy, mommy, mommy, mommy, mommy, mommy, mommy!"

"Connor, slow down before you hurt yourself," Carl Sullivan watched as his son ran through the house chasing Max, trying to grab his tail. "We have to stop feeding that kid in the morning," he said to his wife.

"It's not the cereal. I think he has another secret stash of candy somewhere." Jess took a sip of coffee as the dog ran into the kitchen and hid under the table for protection. The two year old eventually showed up. Both adults stared at him standing naked, arms akimbo in the doorway.

"Billy," Carl called out to his oldest son. "Do you have any idea what happened to your brother's pajamas?"

The eight year old yelled back, "I heard him in the bathroom a minute ago. He was flushing the toilet. They're probably on their way into the sewer system by now like yesterday's underpants."

Carl patted his wife on the shoulder and left the room. He returned with a plunger in his hand to report that the pj's were safely rinsing in the bathtub and fortunately had not gone the way of yesterday's underpants.

"I'm bringing the boys to Wickford this evening. Santa's coming into the harbor by boat and then riding around the village with the kids in a horse drawn cart. I was going to take some pictures for our Christmas cards this year. Do you want me to wait for you?" Jess asked.

"I should be home at a decent hour and we could treat them to dinner at a restaurant."

"Let's plan on getting the picture taken first, though. I bought them the cutest flannel shirts and vests with a reindeer embroidered on the pockets. We'll bring along a change of clothes so they can wear the same outfits on Christmas Day."

"Or we could just let them take their clothes off when we get to the restaurant and eat au naturel," Carl suggested in a voice loud enough to be heard in the living room.

"Ew! That's a sick idea! I am not doing that!" Billy informed his parents as he put on his coat and headed outside to wait for the school bus.

"Your brother won't complain," his father yelled after him before the door slammed shut.

"Both parents had a brief moment to take another sip of coffee before Connor returned to the kitchen with his dripping snowman pajamas draped over his head. He looked down at the puddle forming around him. "I melting, Mommy."

"I think it might be time to bring out Elf on a Shelf," she warned her son. "And somebody needs to have a little talk explaining the difference between naughty and nice," his wife advised her husband as she took the mop from the hall closet.

"I'll put that on the top of my To Do List. He gave her a kiss on the cheek. "I'm going to stop by the hospital on the way to work to see how the Pruitt woman is doing. I'll give you a call before I leave the office. Have fun today!" He patted her on the butt and narrowly escaped being hit with the mop as he headed out the door.

"Buddy, don't forget we're going shopping after school."

"Aunty, I didn't tell you, we have another band practice this afternoon - to get ready for the Christmas concert."

"Well, what time do you expect to get home?"

"I'm not sure. It depends on the tubas. They're always a few notes behind whenever they're supposed to join in."

"I don't see why everybody else has to be there. Has your teacher never heard of a metronome? Turn it on to the correct beat and make the tuba section stay after school until they can keep up! Or have them come in on Saturdays. That should do it!"

"How about we don't give the band director any bright ideas? Some of my best friends are tuba players."

Suzanne laughed as she finished making his sandwich and put it in a bag. "You're getting so big. I thought that suit jacket we bought you last January would fit you for at least two years."

"I could get along with my new blue dress shirt and a tie. I don't need a jacket. Really, Auntie, you're just wasting your money. You could buy something you could use."

"Father Langevin has chosen us to light the Advent candle this Sunday and I want to make sure we look extra nice. Besides, you'll need a decent jacket for the Winter Ball. Have you decided who you're going to ask yet?"

"No one takes dates anymore. A bunch of us are renting a limo and going together. And I'm pretty sure it's casual dress."

Their conversation was interrupted by a knock at the door.

"I'll get it," Evelyn called from the living room. She looked through the peep hole. "It's the police," she informed them as they stood waiting for her to open the door. Suzanne unlocked the bolt and let Sergeant Shwinnard into the room.

He took off his hat. "I won't keep you long, Ma'am, but Detective Sullivan knew you were worried and he wanted me to come by and tell you Mrs. Pruitt seems to be doing better this morning. He stopped by the hospital on his way to work."

"Thank you, Sergeant. Would you like to come in for a cup of coffee?"

"I appreciate the offer, Miss Tetreault, but I'll just be on my way."

After he'd left, Buddy asked, "What was that about?"

"I got a call that Beatrice had gone into cardiac arrest. I rushed over and by the time I got there, they had her stabilized."

"Why didn't you tell me?"

"There was nothing else to do and you were out with your friends and didn't get home 'til later. By that time the emergency was over. No need to worry you about it."

Suzanne looked at Evelyn who quickly changed the subject. "Do you want me to drop you off at school? I don't mind. It'll give us a chance to chat."

"That's okay, I don't feel much like talking."

Both women stood behind the window curtain as he walked slowly along the sidewalk. They watched until they could no longer see him.

Sophia arrived just in time to wave to Stewart as he pulled out of his driveway on his way to an early class. He signaled for her to stop and got out of his car to talk before jumping back into his car and heading off for work.

Kara was in the kitchen doing the breakfast dishes.

"I believe you're the last person left who doesn't use a dishwasher." She gave Kara a hug, took a towel from the hook to dry the cups and saucers in the strainer.

"I enjoy doing this. It gives me time to think while I work."

"Like you don't multi-task enough! I've got a pile of ironing waiting for you in my laundry room when you need more thinking time," Sophia said.

"Hey, those are spiffy looking scrubs you're wearing," Kara admired the dark green pants and top with scenes of children playing in the snow.

"It brightens up the ward. Now's a tough time for a kid to be in the hospital. I've got different holiday scrubs for every day leading up to Christmas."

"I don't doubt it!"

"Oh, here. I have a present for you." She took a box from her bag and handed it to Kara.

Kara unwrapped the present and took out a tie-dyed silk scarf. "This is beautiful, Sophia. And it blends into so many shades of red - my favorite color. Was this from your gift closet?"

"I went to a workshop at Fayerweather House in September. The instructor supplies the materials and you bring home what you make. Next week, Ruth and I are taking a class in crafting sea glass jewelry. I think there are some slots left if you want to sign up."

"Except for my wedding band, I don't usually wear jewelry." She wrapped the scarf around her neck and Sophia helped her to tie it.

"You should wear red more often. Your entire wardrobe is composed of black or grey pant suits. Let's go shopping next week and get you some bright clothes. Ruth needs to buy a few outfits for the honeymoon. We could make a day of it."

"Sounds like a plan."

They finished putting the dishes away. Kara laughed when they got outside. On the front of Sophia's car was a big red nose and antlers were poking up on each side of the roof.

"I bought a bunch on sale after Christmas last year. They were practically giving them away. Gino and Ruth and Rick are all riding around with them. I've got plenty more in my closet. As a matter-of-fact, I just gave Stewart two. He told me he'd misplaced yours. Now, you have a set for both cars."

"Yayyyyy," Kara said weakly, "Just what I've always wanted!"

They stopped by Sophia's house before heading into town. She measured and pinned the maroon velvet dress to be hemmed. "I'm going to let the waist out some. The fit seems snug and we can't be having you holding your breath through the entire wedding. One good thing about this extended vacation you're on is that you've finally gained some weight. Stewart's cooking skills must be improving," Sophia commented.

Kara sighed, "I wouldn't go that far. But he is becoming more innovative. Sometimes I get the feeling our kitchen is just one big science lab."

"There, that's done. I'll work on it tonight," Sophia said. "Be careful of those pins when you take it off. I have the rest of the morning free. What should we do?"

"I thought we might stop into Kenyon's and choose a robe for Beatrice for when she's able to get out of bed," Kara suggested.

"It's a miracle they were able to resuscitate her last night. I don't think she's going to make it to Christmas," Sophia confided to her friend.

"Still, I'd like her to have something nice to wear if she does wake up," Kara said.

"I don't think I'll ever go up those stairs again," Sophia said as they walked through the front door of the department store. "If you don't mind, I'll just wait down here for you."

Kara went to the women's department on the second floor. She chose a soft pink plush robe and a cream colored nightgown with candy canes sprinkled around the bodice and brought the clothes down to the bottom of the staircase to get Sophia's stamp of approval.

When she returned to the first floor, Sophia was at the counter paying for a pair of slippers. "I thought these would go nice with the robe and nightgown."

"What girl doesn't need a pair of red slippers?" Kara agreed.

"Would you like me to buy you a pair? You could click your heels together and wish you were home again," Sophia teased.

"No, I think I'll stay right where I am with my friends." Kara began to sing, "There's no place like home for the holidays."

The clerk handed Sophia her change and the two friends left the store arm in arm harmonizing the tune as they walked to the car.

Vida was beginning to feel the holiday spirit. She unpacked the cartons and hung the wreath on the door. Pouring herself a large glass of fruit punch, she sat down next to the miniature boxwood and began to tie red velvet bows on the ends of the branches. After decorating the tree, she poured herself another drink and tried to remember where the ugly Christmas sweaters were stored. She'd emptied the drawers in the spare room to make room for Sherman's stuff when he first moved in.

She'd never celebrated National Ugly Christmas Sweater Day which fell each year on the third Friday of December. She took out her bucket list and added "December 15 - Wear Ugly Christmas Sweater".

It took some searching until she found them in the antique file cabinet in the attic. She pulled out the one on the top – her favorite. It was purple with a multi-colored reindeer pattern covering the front and back. It was in good condition – no holes - but the smell of mothballs was making her eyes water. Vida took the other sweaters from the drawer and examined a dark aqua with small white crocheted snowflakes running along the sleeves and a gigantic flake on the back. There was a stain on the front but she knew it could be covered up with a fancy bow.

The top drawer held only an unfamiliar brown sweater and as she unfolded it, a manila envelope fell at her feet. In the corner was a label: Sherman Pruitt - Papers. She opened it and looked inside to see if there was any cash. Scanning the sheets, she quickly realized there was nothing of value. Resealing the flap, Vida wrapped it back up in the sweater to give to Evelyn at the funeral on Saturday. Then she went downstairs to decide which ugly sweater to wear first.

Stewart arrived home to find Kara setting the table for dinner. He checked the slow cooker. "You made my favorite – short ribs in your special barbecue sauce."

"Yup. Home-made right from the kitchen of Sweet Baby Rays. They had a sale at Belmont's. A buck a bottle."

He kissed the back of her neck. "I have a surprise for you, too. Guess what's in the bag?"

"I don't have a clue."

"Ta Da!" He presented her with the antlers and reindeer nose.

"Wow! I am speechless!"

"Don't thank me. Thank Sophia. She bought one for each of us. These antlers are even bigger than the old ones we misplaced. I'll just go out and put them on your car. I'll be right back."

"I think I'll call to thank her right now."

After dinner, they washed and dried the dishes and then Stewart changed from his green flannel shirt into his blue flannel shirt before leaving for a Rams basketball game at the university. He found her reading in the den.

"Are you sure you don't want to go?"

"No, I'm not in the mood for crowds tonight. And I want to finish this mystery Ruth lent me. You can read it when I'm done. It's set at URI."

"Now you have my attention. Have you figured out who the murderer is, yet?"

"Of course. I recognized the killer at the end of the second chapter."

"Was it the handsome, brilliant astrophysicist?"

"You'll have to read the book for yourself. Have fun with the guys."

Kara finished the last few chapters thinking all the while she knew the killer's identity and then realized she hadn't guessed right. She was definitely losing her touch. She had a moment of doubt. *Maybe I should get back to work?*

Taking the index cards from the desk drawer, she reviewed her notes from the crime scene. During their evening phone conversation, Sullivan stated that everything seemed to point to Beatrice Pruitt as the murderer. But Kara admitted she still wasn't convinced.

From the closet, she took out the red woolen coat Sophia had picked out for her during their morning shopping spree. It hadn't taken much coaxing from her friend to talk her into buying it. Looking in the hall mirror, she smiled and murmured, "Snug as a bug in a rug." She decided to bring Beatrice her Christmas gift early.

Kara spoke with the head nurse before going to the room at the end of the corridor. She placed her new coat on the chair by the bed. In the small closet were two hangers for the robe and pajamas. She cut off the price tags on the clothes, put the red slippers on the top shelf, and closed the door.

The quiet in the room was broken only by the intermittent soft beeping of the monitor by the bed. Bea slept peacefully, her doll tucked under the covers. Its porcelain face nestled by her breast. Kara sat next to the woman whose life she'd saved – but for what purpose? The world hadn't been kind to Beatrice up to now and her future seemed to hold more of the same. Did the poor woman even want to wake up? Maybe in the past few days she'd given up on life and decided to fall asleep and never awaken again?

Kara hoped she would get another chance to speak with this woman. She had questions – questions only Beatrice Pruitt could answer for her and so she sat waiting patiently in the dark with only the hum from the machines to keep her company.

Saturday, December 2

10

SLEEP IN HEAVENLY PEACE

December had come in like a lamb. The sun shone brightly over the townspeople making final touches for the evening's Winter Wonderland Festival. The store windows were filled with gifts and many displayed home-made gingerbread houses created by the local businesses and organizations for the annual competition. Each store competed for the best window dressing and Gino was the main judge. First prize was dinner at The Towers in Narragansett with the author of a popular local mystery series who would give the winner and the business a shout-out in her next book. Fourteen miniature houses decorated in colored icing and sugar plums were being carefully transported and placed in store windows throughout the village.

Jess fed and dressed the boys then whisked them into the car to take them to the Wakefield Mall to watch Santa arrive for the second time that weekend. This time in a helicopter. Carl slept in for an extra twenty minutes after they'd left until Max realized there was someone else in the house with him and came clambering in to pull the covers from the bed.

"Max! Stop it! Max, Enough! If you don't stop, I'm going to get the boys a cat for Christmas. A mean, old scruffy cat with gigantic, sharp claws."

His warning had absolutely no effect on the puppy who continued to jump and yelp and wag his tail in glee. Carl gave up and decided to take a shower. Max jumped in with him.

He'd used up all of the clean towels to dry the puppy's sopping fur when the phone rang. He ran to answer it with Max following at his heels.

"Hello?"

"You sound a bit flustered," said Kara.

"Just playing with the dog."

"I called to ask if you planned on attending Sherman Pruitt's funeral later this afternoon."

"Ah, a quiet, somber funeral. Count me in. I'll be at the station if you want to come by and we can go together."

"See you around one thirty."

"He hung up and began searching to see what further mischief Max had gotten into. Following the water trail, he found the puppy sound asleep in his crate, exhausted. He gathered the towels and put them in the washing machine then grabbed the mop. As he cleaned up the mess, the idea of returning to the bedroom for a quick nap, flitted through his head.

Gino hauled the over-sized chair from the vault he now used as a storage room at the Courthouse Center for the Arts. He spent an hour re-upholstering it, changing the red velour to blue to match the decor.

At nine o'clock, he turned on the fairy lights and settled into Santa's chair to admire his work. Everything was in place for the crafts fair later that day.

The vendors began arriving, setting up their tables The tired custodian snored through it all until Santa arrived and woke him up.

"Ho, ho, ho! Looks like someone is sleeping in my chair!"

"Hey, Santa! Musta dozed off. You can take over now."

Gino's cell phone rang. It was Sophia asking him when he expected to come home for lunch. She had some errands for him to do. He said he'd be right there and then commented to the jolly, old soul, "I don't know about you, Santa, but dese holidays are killin' me."

Evelyn stood at the entrance of the chapel. Kara and Carl watched as people trickled into the room, spending a minute or so to extend their condolences to Evelyn for her loss. Eight rows of six chairs were facing a speaker's podium with the casket front and center. A young woman was setting up two floral displays on either side.

The scent of lilies brought back memories of her mother's funeral but, unlike that day, Evelyn felt no sorrow. She glanced at the empty chairs, relieved when Rosa Brooks and a small group of people arrived.

A large-bosomed woman wearing a shapeless black coat planted herself directly in front of Evelyn.

"You don't know me. I'm Lucy Goosenik. And these are some of the teachers from the school." She got through half of their names and began to sob, blowing her nose into a soiled handkerchief she pulled from inside her coat sleeve. She clutched at Evelyn's arm. "Sherman and I were such good friends. I can't believe he's gone."

Rosa hastily steered them all into the third row. A sour-faced woman with dark stringy, waste-length hair hastily introduced herself as "Ms. Pinto, Sherman's Secretarial Assistant". She flounced to a seat at the opposite end of the second row away from the others, turning to scowl in their direction. They all began to talk among themselves. She crossed her arms and stared straight ahead.

Vida was next in line. "Now that is one angry beeee-itch," she commented, causing a stir among the teachers.

Carl suppressed a chuckle as Kara nudged him with her elbow. Unphased, Vida turned her attention back to Evelyn. "I almost forgot. I've got an envelope to give you." She patted her oversized pocketbook. "I found it in the file cabinet in my attic. It's Sherm's."

Hyram Harknettal, who was waiting to offer his condolences, inched forward impatiently and Vida took the hint. "I'll give it to you after the service, Evie."

Harknettal introduced himself and asked Evelyn if there was anything he could do to help ease her pain. She assured him she was fine and thanked him for his concern. He seemed ready to continue the conversation, but the minister interrupted to ask for a moment to confer with the family.

"We'd like the service to be simple. A few prayers and a blessing will suffice," Suzanne assured him.

"Will you be speaking, Miss Pruitt?"

"Aside from the fact he was my father, I really have nothing good to say about him, Reverend." Suzanne put her arm around Evelyn and together, with Buddy, they moved to the front seats.

The first bars of Led Zeppelin's "Stairway to Heaven" from the speakers on the wall filled the room. Loud sniffling emanated from the second row. Lucy Goosenik sobbed, "That was Sherm's favorite song."

Vida stage-whispered to the Superintendent sitting in front of her, "At least someone's sorry he's dead."

At the end of the hymn, the minister offered a few general words about the deceased, whom he'd never met, ending with a passage from the Bible and the "Our Father". A recording of Blue Murder's version of "Sleep on Beloved" played and the minister ended the service with a blessing, "And may his soul rest in peace."

Evelyn invited everyone to the church hall for a luncheon.

The people in attendance clustered in small groups before going up to the buffet table. Vida and Rosa stood near the door with Kara and Carl.

"Must be kinda tough for you, Lieutenant Langley. Bein a woman cop, I mean. And black."

To Sullivan's surprise, Kara seemed taken aback for a moment.

Rosa chuckled. "Detective Langley and I had a conversation the other day about being a woman in a job traditionally considered to be a man's domain."

"We do have a lot to commiserate about," Kara agreed, smiling at her friend.

"Uh, no offence, of course," Vida said to Sullivan. "You bein' white and a male."

"No offence taken," he said.

Rosa excused herself to join the other faculty members who were at the buffet table.

"Had you ever previously met any of the people who showed up today?" Sullivan asked Vida.

"I recognized the angry woman from her picture in the school yearbook. Gloria Pinto, his secretary. I remembered her name because of that horsey face. And Ichabod Crane over by the door came by the house once looking for Sherm. I'm not sure about any of the others."

"Did Mr. Pruitt ever say anything that would lead you to believe someone at work wanted him dead?" Carl asked.

"I can't imagine anyone not wanting him dead, especially if they'd been in close proximity to him for long periods of time. He was a real charmer," she added sarcastically.

Evelyn entered the hall and Vida walked over to a table with her. She reached into her bag and brought out the sweater.

"Before I forget, I think this is the last of your father's stuff."

The envelope slipped from the folds of the sweater onto the floor. Harknettal, who was sitting with Porthull and Pinto, ran over to pick it up, then handed it to Vida.

She continued her conversation with Evelyn. "I found this in my attic."

"I appreciate you getting my father's belongings to us, Vida. I doubt if this is of any importance but I'll open it later."

Buddy and Suzanne brought food to the table.

"I made up a plate for you. Sit down and eat."

"Thanks, Suzy, but I'm not very hungry," Evelyn said.

"You have to eat something." She pulled out a chair for her and placed the dish on the table. Evelyn began picking at the food.

"We obviously overestimated Sherm's popularity and ordered way too much. We can send some home with the people who showed up. I brought Tupperware containers with me."

This made Evelyn smile and pat the older woman's hand, "Of course you did."

Rosa left the group of teachers to speak with Kara. "I tried to get more faculty to attend," she said looking at the handful of people sitting at the table. "Certainly not the way I want to be remembered."

Kara agreed. "I'm glad you arranged those interviews for us. It helps put things into context."

"You're welcome. Anything I can do to help, please call or stop by."

"And the same if there's anything I can do for you," Kara said.

119

"Can you arrange to get Harknettal out of my hair for awhile? Maybe put him behind bars on suspicion of whatever. I'm sure if you dig deep enough, he's guilty of something."

Kara laughed, "I'll look into that for you."

When everyone else was busy eating, Kara and Sullivan made their way up to the buffet. Carl glanced at the people sitting around the room. "Looks like the guy didn't have many friends. Do you get a sense any of these people was an enemy? Someone who hated him enough to kill him?"

"I've been watching Harknettal and if I had to hone in on any one of them, it would be him. He has too many prior connections to Pruitt for me to believe it's just coincidence. I know if we search further, we'll find more," Kara replied. "What about you?"

"It took us a while to get some time with Gloria Pinto, but she has an alibi. She was locked up, so that rules her out. The teachers all check out. Since it was the holiday, most of them were at home with their families. Steven Porthull was out of town. That made it easy to narrow down anyone who might have been in the vicinity of Kenyon's on Wednesday night. Vida was alone after she threw him out of the house. She's a woman who definitely could kill someone but I think she was just relieved to get him out of her hair."

"She isn't someone who hides her feelings well. If she murdered him, I think she'd let everyone know." Kara glanced at the large woman in the turquoise sweater with a snowflake on the back and a large orange tassel on the front. "It seems we've established Sherman wasn't Mr. Popularity, but we haven't discovered any compelling reason for killing him."

"I know you don't want to hear this, but Beatrice Pruitt is still my top suspect. She had means, motive, opportunity."

"It doesn't look good for her, I'll admit, but I have a few more questions I'd like her to answer before I can agree with you."

"From what the doctors told me this morning, it looks as though the chance of her regaining consciousness is slim."

"When I was in her room, just before she coded, Bea opened her eyes and looked at me. I had the feeling she wanted to tell me something. I don't think she'll rest in peace until she does."

Buddy approached them with a container in his hands. "My aunt said to give this to you for your boys. We ordered too much food and she's making up some leftovers. Would you like me to get you one, too?" he asked Kara.

"No thank you, I don't have kids at home." Buddy smiled at her and turned to go.

"You're a Yankee's fan, right?"

He didn't answer.

"That's my husband's favorite team. He grew up in New Jersey. I bought him that same cap for his birthday. The one you were wearing at the hospital the other night."

When he turned to face her, his face was flushed. "My aunt gave it to me for having perfect attendance and getting all A's last year."

"She must be really proud of you. I know I'd be."

"Thanks," he muttered and then hurried away to give Rosa Brooks the school yearbooks Suzanne had salvaged from the garbage.

Carl was curious. "What was that about?"

"Sophia saw him in the hospital on Thursday night. He had on that baseball cap and a backpack. He must have come to Beatrice's room when she was sleeping and put the doll in bed with his mother and then covered her with the blanket. I think I need to have a talk with him."

When the mourners had left, Evelyn, Suzanne, Vida and Buddy joined the minister to accompany the body of Sherman Pruitt to his final resting place. Kara and Carl, watched from the parking lot as the pall bearers carried the casket across the grass to the adjacent graveyard. The sun drifted behind grey clouds and a light rain began to fall.

11

FA, LA, LA, LA, LA, LA, LA, LA, LAAAAAAAAAH!

Gino called out to his wife, "Sophia. I need some help here!"
She found him tangled up in the shirt and suspenders from his Santa outfit.

"Gino, stop struggling so I can get the suspenders unravelled. What a mess! I may have to cut you out of this."

"No way, Sophia! The kids are countin on Santa showin up. Ya can't go ruinin da suit!"

His wife finally managed to straighten him out and supervised the rest of his dressing, making him sit still while she laced up the big, black boots.

"Lookit dat shine, Sophia. I worked on it wid real boot black for two hours."

She admired his work and then went into the closet to get out her own caroling outfit. A soft, sea green velvet dress cinched at the waist with a violet satin cummerbund. The matching green velvet cape had a fluffy white fur collar with a muff and Cossack hat to match. Her own stylish leather boots were thigh-high with laces all the way up the front.

"Ooooh la la! You look gorgeous, Sophia. Dose boots are real sexy and I think they're even shinier den mine!" Gino exclaimed admiringly.

"Connor, get into this room so mom can dress you!" Carl said using his most threatening voice.

"Lalalalalalalalalalalalalalalalalalal!" Connor wasn't easily intim-idated. He ran back and forth from one end of the living room to the other with his pudgy fingers stuck in his ears. He'd observed Billy doing this on many occasions when his brother didn't want to listen to what he had to say.

"Let him run around. He's been doing it for the past hour. He'll fall down pretty soon and you can dress him while he's busy crying," Billy advised as he walked through the house in his elf shoes, the silver bells ringing merrily.

"I'm not sure those elf slippers are sturdy enough for walking around the sidewalks," Carl said to his wife.

"The bottoms are leather, so I think he'll be okay."

"Connor get in here so your mother can get you dressed!"

"Lalalalalalalalalalalalalalalalallalalala!" They heard a dull thump and then sobbing coming from the living room.

"See, I told you," Billy informed his parents, smugly.

"Duly noted," his father conceded in a resigned voice.

Jessie grabbed her mug for one last swig before going to tend to the crying child. "Carl, I don't think we're making this coffee strong enough."

Clay Van Zinck was finishing last minute details for the night's caroling when a tall, thin man he didn't recognize, walked into the room.

"May I help you?" he asked.

"I want to join the caroling group."

"We always welcome new singers, Mr. ..." he waited for a name.

"I'm a pretty good tenor. Do you need t-t-tenors?"

"As I said, we're always open to new members who love to sing but I'm afraid we've had our final practice. We'll be performing in an hour or so. We do have a spring concert this April, if you'd like to take part in those rehearsals. They'll begin in ..."

"I'm just interested in Christmas songs. I c-c-catch on real fast." He sang the scale a few times ending with "Do re me fa sol laaaaaaaaaaa ..." at the top of his lungs, bowing low with arms outspread. Then he began to sing a chorus of "Deck the Halls". "See? I d-don't n-n-need to rehearse!"

Clay wasn't sure what to do. He had always prided himself in being the epitome of a southern gentleman and liked to avoid confrontations at all cost - especially if it appeared they may become vulgar. "My, my, my. That was quite nicely done. You have a fine voice, Mr. ... ummmm, um, Sir."

"That's it then. I'm in! Now, I'll just n-need one of your c-c-costumes." He went over to the opened closet and took out a Santa Claus suit. "Looks like this'll d-do just fine with the help of a p-p-pillow or two."

"You'll need to sign for that, Mr. ...."

He grabbed the pen from the choral director and scribbled his name in the book. "Guess I'll see you in t-t-town, then," he called out as he strode from the hall.

"Well, I'll be!" Clay exclaimed. "And La dee da, fiddle dee dee to you too, Sir."

Kara and Stewart had arranged to meet their friends at Meldgies to get something to eat before connecting with the rest of the carolers at the Contemporary Theatre on Main Street. They gave a wave to Ruth, Rick and Sophia when they came into the restaurant.

"Where's Gino?" Stewart asked.

"He's still in the car. He wants to make a grand entrance." Sophia said.

"If you ask me, he's taking this Santa thing a bit too serious," his brother asserted as the two women shook their heads in agreement.

"Ho! Ho! Ho!" All eyes turned as Gino tromped into the restaurant with a satchel thrown over his shoulder. He began plucking sweets and small toys from the bag and tossing them to the people at the counter and then to those at the tables and booths.

"How are we going to live with him? There are still twenty-three days to get through until Christmas!" Ruth looked at them for advice.

Sophia took a small pill box from her purse. "That's what tranquilizers are for," she said shaking the container for added emphasis as her husband began dancing around, leading the customers in a rousing rendition of "Must be Santa! Must be Santa! Must be Santa, Santa Claus!"

They left the restaurant. Gino jumped out into the road in front of Sweeney's Liquors to flag down the South County Trolley which took them the short distance to the theatre where they would start the festivities with the tree lighting and caroling. Luminaries had been placed along the sidewalks to be lit later in the evening. Inside the shops, merchants in costume were preparing to reenact scenes from classic holiday movies.

"Look, there's Carl and Jess and the boys!" Kara waved at the family walking down Kenyon Avenue toward Main Street. The boys began to hop up and down when they caught sight of Santa and to their delight, the trolley stopped so Gino could throw candy and trinkets to them.

"Dis Winter Wonderland is better den Mardi Gras," Gino declared.

"Hey, Billy has the same elf shoes like the ones you misplaced," Stuart pointed out. "I'll have to find out from Jess where I can buy some more."

Kara quickly changed the topic. "Which store window do you think Gino picked for first place? Did he tell you?" she asked Sophia.

"No, he spent the last two nights walking around town taking notes which he's kept hidden somewhere at work." She looked over at her husband waving to the people on the street. "He loves the holidays and is taking these tasks quite seriously. He doesn't want to disappoint anyone, especially the kids."

"I wonder what he'll say when he finds out Arthur is Santa, too."

"Oh, I took care of that." Ruth chimed in. "Arthur has been reassigned to helping with the candy-making demonstration at Sweenor's Chocolates. They gave him a big chef's hat and an official apron. He gets to stir the vat of chocolate and help pour it into molds. And they let him taste test the results. When I told him about the job opening, he turned in his Santa suit to Clay without batting an eye."

"My brother will be the only Santa on Main Street tonight," Rick added, "thanks to my clever fiancée." He gave her a kiss just as the trolley stopped in front of the Contemporary Theatre where other carolers in costume had begun to slowly gather. The friends fell into their places - Sophia with the sopranos, Kara with the altos and Rick and Stewart stood opposite them in the bass section. Gino went to the oversized chair by the tree and sat waiting for youngsters to arrive. They began warming up their voices under Clay's supervision.

"All right everyone, What noise annoys an oyster?"

"A noisy noise annoys an oyster," they responded enthusiastically.

"Who sells sea shells by the sea shore?"

"She sells sea shells by the sea shore," they dutifully called out in perfect unison.

"Everyone," Me,me,me,me,me,me,me. La,la,la,la,la,la,la. Flex your lips and tongues. I want to hear every word loud and clear," he said then added "please" because Clay was always a gentleman.

Hyram Harknettal parked his car in the lot at the elementary school. He put on the Santa hat and adjusted the full, white beard before he got out and crossed the bridge leading to the back of the Block Building. In the darkness, he could hear singing from where the townsfolk were gathered around the tree. He pulled the red felt hat down low over the synthetic wig and headed for the back door leading up to the apartments on the second floor.

The light was on at the top of the narrow staircase. He knocked. No one answered. The lock on the door was no deterrent to him. It gave easily when he pushed the hex key up above the tension wrench and applied pressure. The kitchen smelled of holiday baking. He took a cookie from the platter on the table and nibbled at it while standing in the window looking down on the street below.

On the coffee table in the living room, he found the envelope. Inside were the papers he'd come for. He scanned them and seeing they were all there, he began to tuck them into his shirt. An unexpected sound startled him. Someone had opened the door. Hyram's back stiffened.

"What are you doing here?"

He didn't turn to see who was speaking.

"Did you hear me? Why are you here?" The voice was steady and held no fear.

Hyram ran into the kitchen, out the door, and down the stairs. He could hear footfalls behind him. Clutching the envelope to his chest, he flew toward the river, not daring to look back. In the middle of the bridge a hand grabbed the back of the loose-fitting coat and yanked him to a stop. He was abruptly whirled around, his back pressed against the railing. He looked into the eyes. Angry eyes.

"I asked you a question! What were you doing in my house?"

He tried to push back, dropping the envelope. The strain of the two bodies caused the wooden rails to crack and then give. Hyram felt himself toppling into the icy water.

When he surfaced the first time, he looked up, weakly calling for help. His saturated suit and heavy boots weighed him down as he tried in vain to swim for the nearby water's edge. He went under for the last time and disappeared in the darkness.

On the other side of the fence, the tree in front of the theatre suddenly lit up as everyone joyfully finished the last verse of the song, "Fa,la,la,la,la, La, la, la, la."

Sunday, December 3

12

WHERE ARE YOU CHRISTMAS?

Suzanne and Evelyn were in the kitchen drinking coffee. Buddy came in, planting a kiss on the top of his aunt's head.

"Well, don't you look sharp in your new clothes!" Evelyn exclaimed.

"He's growing so fast, we're going to have to find excuses to go out to fancy places so he can get some use out of them," Suzanne teased. She handed him a box. "I bought you a tie last night. The stores were giving 15% off everything for the holiday shoppers."

"Looks very festive. Thanks, I like it."

"That pattern was pretty tame compared to some of the others. But I thought the green wreaths against the navy background would suit you well seeing as you'll be helping to light the Advent candle today." She helped him knot the tie asking Evelyn, "Do you want to walk or ride?"

"It's not far and the weather's mild. I think we could use a little stroll this morning."

She glanced at the envelope lying next to the sink. "Remind me to open this up and read it when we get home," she said as she helped Suzanne on with her coat.

St. Francis of Assisi was full as many churches tended to be in the weeks leading up to Christmas. They sat in the front pew waiting for the signal to come up and light the purple candle placed with the others inside the greens of the Advent Wreath.

As the choir sang "O Come, O Come, Emanuel", the three came forward. Suzanne and Evelyn recited the words of hope symbolized by the first candle of the Christmas Holy Season. Buddy waited until they were done and leaned over the wreath to light the wick and they blessed themselves and returned to the pew to listen to Father Langevin's sermon about the meaning of Advent.

He looked out upon the congregation, "What should Christmas mean to all of us and what must we do to prepare for the coming of our Savior?"

Buddy and Evelyn sat on either side of her. Suzanne took their hands in hers and smiled up at the priest in the pulpit.

Sophia had an early shift at the hospital. They ate breakfast and Gino put on his coat, giving her a kiss and telling her he was going to spend the day next door. It was the second day of the craft show and he liked being around people shopping for gifts.

"Don't forget, you said you'd come by the hospital to see the kids. I hung your Santa outfit in the closet," she called out, watching him walk over to the Courthouse Center.

When he arrived, he heard the director desperately pleading with someone, "What do you mean you're sick? We hired you for both days. Where can I possibly get a Santa at the last minute? ... No, of course I don't want you spreading germs on the children. Maybe you could use a surgical mask?" She called out to Gino who was now standing in the door of her office, "Gino, does Sophia have some surgical masks at the house? It's an emergency. Can you get one for me?"

"Maryanne, it's okay. Gimme da phone." He took the receiver from her hand and spoke into it, "Don't worry about nuttin. Take da day off, Santa. I got dis covered." He hung up. "Turn on da lights. I'll be right back. Christmas is saved!"

After church service, Ruth and Rick met Stewart and Kara at Mia's for breakfast. The talk was all about the success of Saturday night's festivities. "If I do say so myself, I think the carolers did a great job."

"It's a shame Clay does all that work for just one night. Maybe some of us could get together to go caroling around the neighborhoods next weekend?"

"I think he'd like that idea. I'll be seeing him at Arthur's tonight and I'll ask him what he thinks," Ruth said.

"I wonder if Carl is sleeping in this morning? That two-year- old of his is a handful," Stewart shook his head. "Thank goodness they had him in that harness thingy or they'd still be chasing him around the village right now!"

"He and Jess seem to take it all in stride. But he did mention to me that they were not planning on having any more kids," Kara told them. "I offered to babysit for them on a Friday night if they wanted to go out together."

"Now, that's a true friend," Rick gave her a thumbs-up.

"It's the least I can do. Running a murder investigation at Christmas just seems to be the antithesis of what the holidays should be about."

"I know you can't give us any specific information, but how's he doing with that?"

"The team did a thorough job of narrowing down the suspects, but there are still some issues that need answers. We've talked about not making any decisions on the case until we can speak with Beatrice Pruitt, so the investigation has slowed down a bit." Kara's cell phone rang and she looked at the caller ID. "Speak of the devil. Hi, Carl. I see you survived last night's festivities. Yes? Where? I'll be right there."

The waitress arrived at the table just as Kara put on her coat.

"The good news is that you get two breakfasts," she kissed Stewart. "Complications," she explained to her friends. "A jogger found a body floating in the Saugatucket a few minutes ago. I'll call you when I get a chance."

"Looks like things have gone from a bit slow to warp speed," Stewart commented eating a piece of bacon from his wife's plate as she flew out the door.

The body in the Santa suit was floating face down in the middle of the river. Officers had launched a boat from the water's edge and were by the body when Kara arrived. "Has Harry been called?"

"I did that right before I spoke with you," Carl said. "He asked me if I realized what time it was. Like I can control when we find a body! He was not a happy camper."

"Any idea who Santa might be?"

"Nope. But I haven't got a look at his face, yet. My officers tell me his coat is snagged on something which kept him from floating down stream and over the waterfall."

Someone called from the bridge. "Got something here!"

Kara and Carl moved quickly to where a team of officers were examining a broken railing. "Rope this area off and start dusting for fingerprints," Carl told them.

Kara looked over at the apartment building. "I'm going to leave you here to deal with Harry. I think I'll see if Suzanne Tetreault is awake."

She went around to the front of the building. The street level door was locked and no one answered the bell to let her in. She returned to the back of the building. The ground level door was slightly ajar and at the bottom of the inside staircase she found a torn piece of red cloth snagged on the hand rail. At the top of the stairs, the lock showed signs of being jimmied. Her knock went unanswered. She donned gloves, carefully turned the door knob and let herself in.

"Hello? Is anyone home?" Kara called out loudly as she walked through the kitchen. A half eaten sugar cookie lay on the window sill. A large envelope was by the sink. It felt damp to the touch and the top flap was ripped open. Everything else was neatly in place. She took a small bag from the counter and placed the cookie inside.

"It's Kara Langley. Is anyone home?" She moved through the living room and then checked each bedroom. She was alone in the apartment. Returning to the kitchen, she picked up the envelope, carefully removing the papers to examine them, then putting them back inside the envelope. She left the apartment by the back entrance.

The medical examiner was speaking with Carl when Kara arrived back at the river's edge.

"Good morning, Harry."

132

"Well you got part of that right. It is morning."

"Now Harry, where's your Christmas Spirit?"

"Bah, Humbug!" They watched as Detective Brown helped him into the boat and rowed out to the body

"He's right, you know. Bodies never seem to show up around here at a decent hour," Carl said. "Was Miss Tetreault awake?"

"No one was home. It's Sunday, so I'd guess they're at Mass. We need to get someone into the apartment to gather some evidence. Looks like Santa paid them a visit last night."

Sullivan called Detective Brown over. "The search needs to be expanded to the Bell Block Apartments. Detective Langley will go with you." Brown summoned two officers and cautioned them to be looking for prints in the trodden snow leading to the doorway. Kara gave them additional instructions when they reached the building.

"Collect the red fibers, dust for prints along the walls and the rail and around the door. We'll hold off on inspecting the inside of the apartment until I speak with Suzanne Tetreault."

Church bells rang out and Kara left to circle around to the street side. She didn't have to wait long for them to round the corner from High Street. Upon seeing her, the women picked up their pace with the boy lagging behind. Two police cars came down Main Street and turned into the driveway on the side of the building leading to the back lot.

"Detective Langley. What's wrong?" Evelyn held on to Suzanne's arm, a look of fear in her eyes.

"We should go inside and I'll explain."

Suzanne unlocked the door and the women entered while Kara waited for the boy to catch up. He avoided making eye contact and she held the door open for him to go ahead of her up the stairs.

Once inside the apartment, Suzanne turned to Kara, "Please, tell me what's happened."

"It appears your apartment was broken into, Miss Tetreault. Your back lock was forced."

Suzanne looked around the room. "When did this happen? Was anything taken? We were all at church."

"I believe it happened some time last night or early morning. Could you tell me where you were?"

"Last night? Evelyn and I went to the tree lighting and then we strolled around and shopped. We took part in the scavenger hunt. We both got in around ten thirty."

"This may have happened while you were out." She turned to Buddy who was leaning against the wall by the door. "What time did you get in?"

"I'm not sure."

"Were you here when they got home?"

He hesitated, "Yes, I heard them come in. I was in my room working on an English project. Evie came to say goodnight."

"He was at his desk. I brought him a snack," she said.

"Why would anyone break in here? We don't have anything of value. There's nothing to take!" Suzanne told her.

"Miss Tetreault. A body was found this morning, behind the building. We have reason to believe he was in your apartment last evening."

Suzanne clutched the edge of the chair. "My God! Another body!"

"Do you have any idea who it is?" Evelyn asked.

"Not yet."

"Buddy, did you hear anything while you were in your room?"

The boy shook his head, "No."

"When you came home, did you come in by the back door?"

"Buddy doesn't use that door. Ever!" His aunt exclaimed.

"So, you wouldn't have seen anyone hanging around by the river's edge?" Kara continued keeping her gaze on the boy.

"Buddy never goes back there. He's deathly afraid of water," Evelyn explained.

"Is that true, Buddy?"

"Yes," the boy's voice was a whisper.

"His stepfather used to punish him by holding his head under water when he was taking a bath. He wouldn't even cross the bridge when he was at the elementary school. I had to walk him around to High Street to get to school every day," his aunt told Kara.

"You're afraid of the river, Buddy?"

"Yes," he answered, his head bowed.

Kara looked at Evelyn. "I believe the intruder may have been after the envelope on the kitchen sink."

Suzanne went to the kitchen and brought it back, giving it to Kara. "Have you read the information inside?"

"No, Vida gave it to me yesterday at the service."

"Would you mind if I took this to be examined? I'll make sure the papers get back to you."

"No, go ahead," Evelyn said.

"So, you think this has to do with Sherman's murder?" Suzanne asked.

"I do," Kara admitted. "My team is outside and they'll need to come in to take some prints. Would you check to see if any valuables were taken?"

The two women went to their bedrooms. As the boy moved to leave, he looked at Kara. She gently touched his arm.

"We need to have a talk." She gave him her card.

He nodded and put it in his jacket pocket

Harry was standing over the body with Carl when she joined them. "No marks on the body, to indicate a struggle. He had a large pillow under the suit. Any injuries will show up once the body thaws. I'll run a tox screen to see if he may have been drinking. Make sure you have someone look at the railing to see if it was strong enough to hold his weight if he went up against it. It could have been accidental. He probably went into the water some time last evening. I'll know better when I do the postmortem. His belt buckle got tangled on a post under the water. It kept him from floating downstream and over the falls."

The beard and wig had been removed and Kara knelt to get a good look at the remains of Hyram Harknettal. She stood up and brushed the snow from her slacks.

"You don't seem surprised," the medical examiner said.

"I've just been talking with the family. The team is inside the apartment collecting evidence. Here, this cookie should be checked for Harknettal's DNA and this is the envelope Vida gave Evelyn at Pruitt's memorial service. The information inside may help us figure out a motive. Appears it may have been taken from the apartment and my guess is Hyram Harknettal wanted the information inside badly enough to break and enter."

"We'll need to bring them in for questioning," Sullivan said.

"I'm going to the hospital. I'll call you if I find anything out," Kara told him.

The bells in the Episcopal Church across the street began to chime. Harry oversaw the placing of Hyram Harknettal's body into the van. He started to walk away.

"Harry, your car's right here," Carl reminded him.

"Don't you think I know where my own car is? Since I'm up early on a Sunday morning, I may as well go to Mass."

Carl gazed at him in surprise. "I thought you were an atheist?"

"I am. But even atheists go to church sometimes. We're not heathens, you know."

Kara went to the children's ward first. Sophia was dispensing juice to some of the little ones who were able to leave their beds. Her bright gold hospital scrubs were patterned with rocking horses and teddy bears.

"You're up and about early for a Sunday morning. I thought you said you and Stewart were going out to breakfast?"

"We met Ruth and Rick at Mia's. But I had to leave before I could eat. Can I have some of that juice?"

"Sure. Do you want me to get you an egg? I'll have them make it over light."

Kara made a face. "No thanks. I couldn't bear the sight of a runny egg yolk at the moment. Do you have any crackers around?"

Sophia moved quickly to wipe up some juice that had spilled on the floor and to comfort the child who'd spilt it. "There, there.

Everything's all right. Look, all gone. Do you want another juice? I'll see if I can find a sippy cup and then you can drop it all you want." The tears turned to whimpers as Kara followed Sophia to the nurse's station.

"Take a couple of these juice boxes and some saltines. You shouldn't be going without food," Sophia chastised her. "Why did you have to leave the restaurant? Wait! Don't tell me. Carl Sullivan called and there's another murder for you to solve."

"Sophia, you're psychic."

"No, I'm not. Someone phoned the hospital about the police finding Santa in the Saugatucket. I'm not sure why the call was routed to our desk. She wanted to know if 'the dead guy' was her husband because he hadn't come home from a Christmas party last night. Imagine! He was their designated 2017 Santa. I assured her, no dead Santa had shown up, and if he had, I would know. She thanked me and I swear she sounded disappointed."

"This morning a jogger discovered the body and Carl called me in to help. He had a feeling it might be connected to the Pruitt murder."

"And what does your instinct tell you?"

"There's no doubt in my mind it is. Have you heard any more about Beatrice's condition?"

"When I went to check her this morning, the nurse on duty told me she'd had a good night. Are you going up to the room?"

"I thought I'd sit with her for a while."

"If you're still there when I have my lunch break, I'll treat you to a meal in our cafeteria."

"Sounds like a good deal to me." Kara hurriedly left her friend as a puddle of apple juice oozed toward her spotless white nurse's shoes and two more crying children were howling for sippy cups, too."

Compared to the children's ward, Beatrice's room was a quiet refuge. The doll was still cradled against her and the monitors kept up a steady hum and beep. Kara pulled a chair up by the bed.

"Hello, Beatrice. It's Detective Langley. Kara," she whispered. "I need to talk with you, so please try to get better." Kara thought she saw a slight flicker of her lids. "I found the note you left in your coat. The one that said you wanted to die because you killed Sherman. I'm not sure I believe you. That's why we have to talk. I saw Buddy this morning. He was all dressed up for church. You would have been very proud of him. Beatrice, I know you can hear me. Wherever you are, please come back."

Sophia came in an hour later. "Let's put some food in you and you can tell me all about your latest adventure. I can't understand why you just don't get back on the job. You have to realize by now that people like you and me are indispensable. The place falls apart without us!"

They laughed as the elevator door opened and the sounds of Alvin and the Chipmunks pleading, "Christmas don't be late" floated out into the hall.

"I wonder how many kids are begging for hoola hoops this Christmas?" Kara said as they stepped inside.

"More like smart phones and drones," Sophia answered.

"Ah, where are the simple Christmases of yesteryear?"

They sat in a quiet corner of the bustling cafeteria and Kara filled Sophia in on the scene at the river. "I got a look at the outfit. It was exactly like Gino's and had that funny label Clay uses to mark all of his costumes."

"I don't remember seeing another Santa anywhere near the tree lighting. I'd have steered them away if I had. Gino would have been crushed. He loves playing Santa. He kept his outfit so he could visit the children's ward this afternoon and spread some cheer. I'm going to buy him his own Santa outfit as a Christmas gift. I found some gorgeous red velour ones on line." She stopped to take a large bite out of her ham sandwich.

"You know, it may have been the costume Arthur had been given. The one Ruth cleverly persuaded him to turn back in." Kara said. "I wonder where she got that idea?"

"I don't think I should feel a bit guilty about that. Arthur had the best time at Sweenor's stirring the chocolate and handing out free samples. They may hire him part-time in February to get ready for the Valentine's Day rush."

"I left Clay a message on his home phone to call me when he gets in this morning. He's probably gallivanting around with some of his friends. They like to go out to eat after the church coffee hour."

"Sometimes he doesn't check his messages. You should stop by the house on your way home," Sophia said.

"I intended to spend some time with Beatrice ..."

"Kara, if she regains consciousness, the nurses will make sure I know and I'll call you right away."

"Thanks, Sophia. I probably will do that."

They returned to the room and nothing had changed.

"You need to accept the fact that she may never wake up, Kara. You'll have to figure out the case from the information Sullivan and the team have gathered." Sophia left her to return to the children.

Softly, she brushed the woman's forehead with her fingertips. "Beatrice, you have to fight a little harder. I need you to help me do the right thing. I don't want to make another mistake. Please, Beatrice."

13

ALL I WANT FOR CHRISTMAS IS MY TWO FRONT TEETH

K ara didn't have far to look when she reached Kingston. The three friends were strolling along the brick sidewalk, arms laden with packages. She pulled into a parking space and opened the passenger side window. They gathered around squeezing together to greet her.

"Kara, what a nice surprise."

"We've been shopping."

"We're not done yet. We still have to stop in at Fayerweather House."

She'd forgotten the tiny village was celebrating Christmas in Kingston. Helme House, the Kingston Hill Store and the library all had sales going on.

"Look, I got a bag of books at the library for five bucks!" Arthur crowed, proudly holding up his satchel.

"There's a great cookie sale going on at the church. Those women know how to bake," Samuel declared.

"Keep eating all that sugar and you'll be losing the few teeth you have left," Arthur warned.

"What are you talkin about, Man? I got more teeth in my head than you do," he shot back.

She interrupted their playful banter, "Clay, I need to ask you something. It's important."

"Sure Kara, we can go to my place and these two can carry on their stimulating discussion without me."

He got into the front seat of the car and waved as his two friends moved on to the crafter's guild.

"Clay, do you remember who you gave the Santa outfits to?"

"Sure thing. Gino and Arthur got their costumes the night of the rehearsal. But Arthur returned his. I hung it in the armoire at the hall. Oh, but the strangest thing happened as I was getting the music packed to take to the tree lighting. A man came in wanting to sing with us. I told him he couldn't because we had already rehearsed. But he insisted and grabbed the Santa outfit."

"Did you recognize him?"

"I thought he seemed familiar and I didn't want to be rude."

"So, you let him take the outfit?"

"I did, but I made him sign for it."

"Can we stop at the Tavern Hall Club and look at the sign-out book?"

"I don't see a problem with that."

They drove the short distance to South Road and parked in the lot behind the hall. Inside visitors were being given tours of the historic Colonial structure built in 1738 by Elisha Reynolds and now owned by the Tavern Hall Club.

Clay and Kara stopped in the billiard room to listen to a club member who was narrating the history of the famous meeting house. "During the American Revolution, Colonel Thomas Potter led the Kingston Reds, our Rhode Island Militia who used this building as a meeting place. In 1781, George Washington along with Alexander Hamilton visited Colonel Potter on the way to Newport to plan the siege of Yorktown with General Rochambeau. In later years, among other uses, it was a general store; an office for the first South County newspaper, the Rhode Island Advocate later to become the Narragansett Times; a boot and shoe company; a women's boarding house; and millinery store owned by Orpha and Elizabeth Rose. The Rose sisters also lent out books from the house which later became the nucleus for the book collection at the Kingston Free Library just across the street."

Moving on to the back of the inn, Clay went to the closet, took out the costume register and opened it. "Ms. Moore was in charge of collecting the clothes at the end of the night so we can send them out to be cleaned. Some people arranged to bring them back to her this morning. See? Look! Here's his signature."

He pointed to the bottom of the page. Kara could just make out the name: Ebenezer Lennox Scroggie.

"Oh, good gracious! It appears Mr. Scroggie has yet to return his Santa suit! They're quite expensive, you know. Red velveteen with a white plush lining and you can't get black leather belts like that anymore. It's an antique. Mercy me! I should have run after him and gotten his number."

"Can you describe him?"

"He was tall and thin and his skin was pale. Oh, I noticed his teeth were somewhat discolored and the front ones were uneven - chipped, I think?"

"What did he say to you?"

"He asked me to let him sing in the chorus that evening. He wouldn't take 'No' for an answer. His behavior was quite uncouth, insisting he was a good tenor. Before I could stop him, he'd grabbed the suit."

"Well, I have some good news and some bad news for you."

"Oh, my goodness. Give me the good news first."

"I know where your Santa suit is."

"Why, that's wonderful, Kara. Everyone says you're a fantastic detective. You could solve any problem."

"Thank you, Clay. I appreciate hearing that."

"What's the bad news then?"

"It's being taken to the forensics lab."

"Lordy me!"

"It was found on a body floating in the river this morning."

"Well, I'll be." He shook his head. "Poor Mister Scroggie! I do believe he had a good excuse for not returning it, then."

"I'll make sure you get it back after the investigation is done although, I'm not sure how long it's going to take."

"Well, thank you Kara. That would be fine."

"You're welcome Clay, but I would guess it's going to be one heck of a dry cleaning bill!"

She drove him to Fayerweather House. Once the home of a freed slave who was the village blacksmith, it was now owned by the Kingston Village Association. Artists from the area sold their crafts and the three rooms that comprised the shop were all decked out for the holidays. Samuel and Arthur were munching on cookies and drinking warm cider in front of the fieldstone fireplace while their gifts were being wrapped in tissue paper and bagged.

"Do you want me to drive you home? You've got a lot of bundles to carry."

"We'll be fine. It's just next door," Samuel assured her.

She browsed around the rooms looking at jewelry, woolen hats and scarves, wooden toys, aprons, and quilts. Tiny, lace baby booties caught her eye and she was looking for a matching cap when her cell phone vibrated.

"Kara! Thank God you answered!'

"Sophia? Is it Beatrice? Is she ..."

"It's Gino. He never showed up. Something's wrong! He would never let the children down! I know something terrible's happened to him!"

"Sophia, calm down. Have you tried his cell?"

"He's not answering. I left texts and a dozen messages. He always picks up even if there's no caller ID. He'll talk to anyone! I'm at home and his car is in the garage. I went over to the Arts Center, but he's nowhere to be found! I phoned Rick. He's watching the basketball game on TV with Stewart. He says they haven't seen Gino today. They're on their way."

"I'll be there in five minutes."

"Kara, You don't think some psycho is running around killing Santa Clauses, do you?"

"Sophia, calm down. Take a deep breath. We'll figure this out. We'll find him."

When she arrived, Rick was walking around the outside of the house. "Sometimes he goes up on the roof when he thinks Sophia has something for him to do, but I looked and the ladder is still in the shed. His car's in the garage." Rick told her. "Stewart's checking the cellar and Ruth and Sophia are doing another sweep of the house."

They went inside and Sophia greeted her with a hug. "I'm so glad you're here."

"Okay, let's start with the last time you saw or heard from him." Kara said.

"We ate breakfast together this morning. He kissed me and said he would be next door at the Arts & Crafts Show. I reminded him about coming to see the kids and then I left for the hospital right after that. When he didn't show up, I called his cell. He didn't answer. I texted a ton of messages."

"So, he left the house. Is there any sign he returned?"

"The clothes he was wearing this morning are in the bedroom and the Santa suit is gone. He has to have come back to change. I looked for a note, but there's none. And his car is still in the garage just where we parked it last night when we got home from Wakefield."

Kara went through the house, opening closets. On the bed were his clothes. "You said you went next door and he wasn't there."

"Maryanne was in her office getting ready to lock up. She said the Santa they'd hired got sick and Gino volunteered to fill in. He spent the morning in the big oak chair asking kids what they wanted for Christmas."

"That's where we need to go next," Kara said.

They walked across the yard and the parking lot. Maryanne was standing at the door waiting for them. "I've looked all over the building and there's no trace of him."

Kara instructed the men to go into the cellar and Ruth and Sophia began another check of the first floor rooms. She went upstairs with the director. "Let's start from where he spent the morning," Kara said.

The twinkle lights around the room were sparkling. The blue velvet cushioned chair was empty, a red sack by its side. Kara walked to the middle, took out her cell phone and dialed Gino's number. The sound of "I Saw Mommy Kissing Santa Claus" came from beneath the chair. Inside the sack, she found the phone. Messages from Sophia filled the screen. Then, a call from Rick's number and the last from Kara.

"Do you notice anything different in here, Maryanne?"

"No, everything looks just like he had set it up. I took pictures. I'll get my iPad and show you." She ran downstairs leaving Kara alone to survey the holiday scene. Icicles, birch trees, mounds of snow, seals, frolicking polar bears, snowmen.

Maryanne returned and they examined the photos. The dim lighting gave everything a dark tone. "Sorry, they're not as clear as I thought they'd be," she said.

Kara sat on the platform next to the white bears. She'd loved those commercials although she wasn't a big soda drinker.

"Where do you store all this stuff?" she asked.

"In the cellar with other sets we use during the year. I opened every door to see if I could find him, but no luck. It's kind of creepy down there. I always thought it would make the perfect setting for a murder," she said just as Ruth and Sophia joined them.

Sophia let out a high-pitched scream on hearing Maryanne's comment.

Ruth took her by the arm and sat her in the oak chair. "It's going to be all right. Don't let your imagination get the best of you, Sophia," she consoled her and turned to Kara for support. But Kara had begun to touch the figures next to her and looked carefully at the photos once again.

"I remember this commercial. One of the bears is missing." She pointed to the screen. "Right there. The biggest one isn't here." She stepped into the space where it should have been.

"Did you see any polar bears when you searched the cellar?" she asked Rick and Stewart who had just come upstairs.

"No Gino. No polar bears," Stewart said causing Sophia to moan.

"Do you know where they're usually stored?" she asked Maryanne.

"They're collectors' items. Gino brought them from his house for the display. I don't think Gino would put them in the cellar with the other stuff. If he decided to store them here, he'd put them some place more secure. You know, there's an old vault on the first floor. It's always locked but I think I have the combination somewhere in my office."

It took some time for her to find it in the piles of papers that had accumulated on her desk. She knelt by the vault and dialed in the combination, listening to the tumblers. Pushing down on the heavy brass lever, the door swung open.

"Jeeze, Louise! I taught you'd never find me!" Gino sat huddled in the corner next to the missing polar bear, his teeth chattering from the cold. "What took youse so long? I'm half stahved! Good ta see youse all! What's for dinna?"

Rick and Stewart pulled him to his feet and Sophia threw her arms around him. She kissed him on the lips. "What would you like, Honey?"

"I could go for a coupla lobstahs," he told her.

"Lobster it is!" Rick declared as the relieved band of friends headed next door.

Thursday, December 7

14

Baby, It's Cold Outside

A storm had traveled up the east coast late Wednesday night. Snow and wind gusts, combined with frigid air, were severing the bare branches of red maples and toppling white pines. Schools and businesses closed and emergency vehicles were kept busy all Thursday morning. Sullivan's face lit up when Kara came into the office.

"Hey! What are you doing out in this? I thought you'd be home with Stewart in front of the fireplace reading a mystery and sipping green tea."

"I knew you'd be on your own here with everyone being sent out on emergencies. Stewart dropped me off. He didn't want me driving in the snow. He's become very protective lately."

"The wires are down at the top of Tower Hill. None of the traffic lights in the area are working and we're getting more reports of outages every hour. Leo is swamped with calls."

"A branch fell on our shed and I'm sure there'll be more to follow before this all ends. But, on the bright side, Stewart is happy because he'll have lots of firewood to chop in the spring."

"Ever the optimist," Carl said. He pointed at the folders of evidence accumulating on his desk. "I think we've interviewed everybody who lives in this town," his voice was weary. "I just need to put all this into some context and get a clear picture of how these two murders are connected. Feel free to jump in," he said. "Here are the coroner's reports on both men."

Kara sat down and began to read the files.

"What do you see?" Sullivan asked.

"In both cases there was a struggle, but no apparent injuries on either except for slight markings around Pruitt's neck. No fingerprints were lifted but fibers were extracted from the weapon used to kill Pruitt suggesting the use of gloves." She looked closely at the reports. Gloves would infer premeditation, but it's winter and possibly the murderer was wearing them before meeting up with the victims." She took an index card and wrote down the fiber information.

"Cause of death with Pruitt was a puncture to his spinal chord with the spindle from the counter. The weapon was already at the scene and close at hand. Harknettal's death was ruled a drowning. It appears there may have been a struggle and he fell from the bridge. Again, no evidence of premeditation."

"Are you thinking that both these deaths could be ruled accidental?"

"It's certainly a possibility but until we know motives and details, we can't assume anything." She said.

"And no 911 calls came through. In Pruitt's case, death was instantaneous, but Harknettal possibly might have been saved if he'd been given CPR," he answered.

"There could be more than one killer," she suggested.

"I'd thought of that. Harknettal appears to have a motive for wanting Pruitt out of the way." He handed Kara the file they'd taken in evidence from Suzanne Tetreault's apartment. "The DNA was Harknettal's. He must have badly wanted what was in that envelope. Enough to go to the store and intimidate Beatrice when he thought she had it. We figure he'd misunderstood. When Pruitt mentioned his ex having the papers in a file cabinet, he was referring to his ex-girlfriend, Vida, not his ex-wife. And when Harknettal saw Vida giving Evelyn the file at the funeral, he realized he had to take the chance of retrieving it from the apartment. He probably followed them home after the service."

"I'm going to go through this with a fine-tooth comb. I'd like to see the boxes with Sherman's stuff that you took from Suzy's place and your notes from the interview we had with Harknettal."

Wind howled outside and the switchboard in the outer office kept ringing as the two partners worked together on the case.

"Gino, get up! How can you sleep through this?" Sophia sat on the edge of the bed staring at the figure under the covers.

Like a turtle, he poked his head out from under the red and white striped quilt. "Sophia, lemme sleep. I had a harrowin experience this week. I coulda died."

"Enough milking the traumatic experience, Gino. Get up and put gas in the snowmobile. You have to get me over to the hospital. They're short-staffed. People are having a tough time driving in to do their shifts. Roads are a mess and the plows can't keep up. Put on your Santa suit! I have a feeling if the parents can't manage to visit, the kids are going to need a little of your Christmas cheer."

On hearing the words, "Put on your Santa suit", Gino threw off the covers and jumped out of bed. "I'll be ready in a jiff!"

"I'll pack some clothes in your Santa bag in case we have to stay overnight," she told him.

"And, could you make me an egg and sausage sandwich for the road? I'm stahved!"

Ruth and Rick stood in front of the window facing South Road watching the snow drifts pile up outside. "I don't think we'll be going anywhere for a day or so," Rick assessed the situation.

"Kara and Sophia and I were supposed to shop for clothes today, but it got canceled. None of the stores are open," Ruth said

Rick laughed. "When did that ever stop my sister-in-law? I'm surprised she doesn't have you both on Skype arranging an internet shopping spree."

"I'm not sure where she finds all of her energy. Have you been in their house lately?"

"Gino escorted me through one day while Sophia was working. He was thinking of selling tickets. Putting a sign outside offering tours when she's away at work."

"Oh, no! Sophia would strangle him!"

"You'll be happy to know I didn't encourage his latest entrepreneurial idea."

"It is decorated beautifully, I have to admit."

"I'm just glad you're easily satisfied with one tree and of course the mistletoe," he told her.

"I think it was a nice addition to the décor. You know, I never really needed mistletoe until I met you."

She waited for Rick to respond with a kiss, but he was distracted at that moment by something outside in the street. A dog came into view, teeth bared and barking furiously as it tried to latch on to the pant cuffs of a Santa on a snowmobile madly kicking at the animal while increasing his already breakneck speed.

They watched fascinated as the vehicle roared past their front yard with Sophia on the back, a red bag thrown over her shoulder, merrily waving at them. By the time they'd raised their hands in response, the dog had given up and sat panting in the middle of the road and the snowmobile with the jolly couple on board had disappeared into the distance.

The phone lines were down in Exeter, but Vida managed to reach Evelyn with her cell. "How's it going in your neck of the woods?" she asked.

"It looks like a ghost town," Evelyn replied, moving the curtains back to see if any car tracks had appeared since the last time she'd checked.

"This could continue until late tonight. At least you're on a main road. Out here in the woods, we'll never dig out."

"Will you be okay?"

"Sure, I got plenty of food and I cut a ton of wood for the woodstove. It'll be cabin fever that gits me, though. I like to be out and about."

"Vida, stay close to home. What if you were to slip and hurt yourself? Nobody would know until too late. You could freeze to death. Look at what happened to Bea."

"Don't worry about me, I'm fine. How is Beatrice?"

"They give us a report from the hospital twice a day and she doesn't seem to be responding since her heart attack," Evelyn answered.

"It don't look good, does it?"

Evelyn looked toward Buddy's room and whispered, "No, it looks pretty bad. Just a matter of time before ..." She stopped herself.

"I been keepin myself busy cleaning things out and if I find anything else of Sherm's, I'll get it to you."

"Thanks, Vida. I'm going to call you tonight before I go to bed to make sure you're inside and safe."

"Okay, I think my cell will have enough charge to get me through tomorrow. Give my regards to Suzy and Buddy."

"That was Vida. She was making sure we're okay," Evie explained as she moved to stand next to Suzanne. They gazed out the window at the tracks in the snow leading from their front door, across the road and up Kenyon Avenue toward Beatrice's house and the hospital.

It took him almost fifteen minutes to make it up the hill to the house. He found the key and let himself inside, checking to make sure the thermostat was set high enough to keep it warm. He turned on the faucets to drip, hoping to prevent the pipes from freezing. In the cellar, he checked the oil tank then found an old shovel he could use to make a path from the front door to the car. He wiped the mounds of snow from the car and then used the keys she kept over the visor to start it up. He let it run for a time, while he cleared the rest of the front path. Returning the shovel to the cellar, he locked up the house and turned off the car engine, replacing the keys.

He continued his journey up the hill to the hospital and went through the front door of the older section of the building. Taking the elevator up, he slipped into the hall and waited. When no one was around, he went into the room and stood over the bed, making sure the blanket was tucked neatly in place and the doll was by her side. He moved the chair by the wall to make a space for him behind it where he couldn't be seen. He sat hunched in the corner waiting for her to wake up. The sound of the machines filled the room as the snow beat against the icy-glazed window panes.

The lights flickered then went off. They stopped what they were doing and waited until the generator kicked in. Index cards were stacked on either side of her chair. Kara had been adding to the piles all afternoon.

Sullivan had made use of the wall space to post photos and notes on what he'd deemed important to each murder.

"Most of my evidence points to Beatrice Pruitt as the killer of her ex-husband, Sherman. If we could establish motive for Hyram Harknettal, I would seriously put him in contention for the murder. Now that his wife has changed her story, it's clear he had the opportunity.

Mrs. Harknettal admitted she'd lied in her first interview when she said her husband was with her the whole time. Actually, they slept in separate bedrooms and she can't confirm his whereabouts later that night. She did tell us that he and Sherman had been good friends for years. Hyram led us to believe they met when he was an administrator in the school where Pruitt was a custodian. The wife confirmed he had little social contact with Sherman at that time."

Kara added, "I've compared their resumes and where their lives intersected at other times before they ended up working together at Mercy Brown. And Rosa told me it was Harknettal who hired Pruitt for the assistant principal position. What was Hyram trying to hide from us?"

"His references all checked out. What do you think is at the root of the deception?"

"I believe Pruitt was blackmailing Harknettal and if we keep digging we'll figure out what he had on him."

"You mean he was an extortionist in addition to being a wife and child abuser?"

"Harknettal was an abuser, himself. His wife was afraid of him. He threatened her in order to ensure she'd give him an alibi." Sullivan pointed to the corrected statement hanging on the wall. "But no one can place him at the store that night."

"No one saw Beatrice at the store either," Kara said.

"So, both have means and opportunity. Beatrice has a motive in that Pruitt abused her and her child, ultimately causing her to lose custody. And as of now, we haven't nailed down what Harknettal's motive could have been although blackmail is a possibility."

Kara picked up the index cards next to her right foot. "We can't rule out some of the other people we've questioned. Pruitt's been described as a bully who enjoyed harassing women."

"But all of the people who've worked with him had solid alibis for Thanksgiving night," he reminded her.

"And then there's Vida. She spent the night alone after she kicked him out. But we both agree she doesn't have a strong motive and she isn't one to hide her true feelings." Kara began looking through her notes.

"I felt we were finally winding up the inquiry. Now Harknettal's death has opened up a whole new avenue to pursue. Was he killed by the same person or by someone avenging Pruitt's death? Or was it an accident?"

"The broken rail could indicate a struggle, I agree. That doesn't rule out it being an accident. But if he was left to drown, if someone was there and chose not to call for help ..." Kara didn't finish her thought. "The question we need to ask is 'Did he have an accomplice with him or did someone in the apartment - Suzanne, Evelyn, Buddy - walk in and confront him?'"

"But wouldn't they call the police if they'd walked in on a thief who then ran from the building? I don't see Evelyn taking chase. But Suzanne is very protective of them and she isn't easily intimidated. I can see her taking things into her own hands and going after someone who broke into her home," Sullivan said.

"And then there's Buddy."

"You think he knows something he's not telling, don't you?"

"There's a lot of anger and fear inside him," she said softly.

"I'm not sure Jess and I know what we're doing sometimes, but I hope we're doing the best we can to raise our two boys to be caring young men. Parenting is hard under the best of circumstances."

"You're fantastic parents! Billy and Connor are amazing boys. You protect them and give them love. But, never to know your dad, to be abused by your stepfather, to have a mom who can't take care of you. It doesn't seem fair to me that some kids really have to fight against the odds just to survive their own family situations."

"Suzanne's been there for him. She's protected him and given him a good life and it's obvious she loves him. I really admire that woman," Sullivan said.

"Yes, she's taken the place of his parents and raised him to be a caring young man. But it can't be easy for him with his mother so close by yet so distant. Who knows what's going on inside him? It's a lot for any kid to deal with."

"He seems like a really nice boy. But who knows what that kind of abuse can do to a kid?"

"I don't understand why men need to bully others."

"It's simple, some guys are insecure, ignorant and feel entitled to use their physical power to give them the feeling of superiority. Even if the people they threaten are vulnerable women and children."

"I'm surrounded by men who would never think of hurting a child. It's alien to me." Kara shook her head as she began to look through the papers on her desk. "You've already spoken with the people listed as references. You take Pruitt and I'll start with Harknettal. Let's see if we can find other sources besides the ones on these resumes."

"My cousin is a detective on Cape Cod in the town where Harknettal worked as the special ed director and where Pruitt was a custodian. I'll start there if you'll call the contacts you have in Louisville from our last case," Sullivan suggested. "That blogger who gave you all the files on the Waddington couple would be a good place to start."

"If anyone can get information, it would be him." Kara placed a call to Alan Ordaway. They caught up on the latest news and when she asked for the information she needed, he said he'd email what he could find out immediately. Then she phoned Stewart.

"Hi, Honey. How's everything at the Public Safety Complex?" he asked.

"By the sound of the phone calls coming in, all of the police and emergency vehicles must be stretched to the limit. How are you doing out there in the woods of West Kingston?"

"I'm glad we bought that generator last fall. We lost power two hours ago. Good you called me on my cell. I've been using the gas stove to cook us up some soups and stews to get us through the week. I've used just about everything in the refrigerator. Wait until you taste my Guess What It Is Stew! I may just have to patent the recipe."

She stifled a groan. "It sounds like you're keeping busy. Maybe when the road gets plowed, you could bring some of that food to the neighbors?"

"That reminds me, when I pick you up, I need to stop and buy some more Tupperware containers."

"Not a bad idea but I don't think any of the stores are open."

"I may have to start using some of those beakers I've got stored in the basement."

She rolled her eyes at Sullivan. "What I called you about was I need you to use your contacts at the university to find me some information on Sherman Pruitt and Hyram Harknettal. They were enrolled at the university in the education program. I'll email you more to go on."

"Do I get my own detective badge?"

"I have a Sheriff's Deputy badge somewhere. It's tin."

"That'll be mighty fine, Ma'am."

"Ah, your John Wayne impression. I haven't heard that in quite awhile," Kara slapped her forehead with the palm of her hand and Sullivan, who'd been listening in, laughed.

"Yup! I gotta go down to the root cellar and round up summa them glass containers to store more victuals. See you later, Little Lady. And don't go takin any wooden nickels."

She hung up. "I may be staying here tonight," she announced.

Christmas tunes filled the corridors of the children's ward. Little ones sat in a circle on the floor listening as Santa read them their favorite holiday stories. A table had been set up with colored paper, crayons, paste and all kinds of decorations. Sophia was helping a little girl in a nightgown with purple unicorns to make a construction paper garland of reds and greens. The smell of popcorn permeated the room with more kernels being eaten than strung.

Amid all of the festivities, Sophia recognized the teen-age boy with a Yankee's baseball cap looking in at them from the hall. She waved to him and he came to the table hesitantly.

"Hello, would you like to join us? I think the children could use some help cutting out the tinfoil for the stars."

He took off his cap and jacket and sat with two young patients in wheelchairs, helping to trace the stars on the foil with a magic marker. A volunteer in a candy-striped uniform brought three large bowls of popcorn to the table and placed one in front of him. He waited until the other children had taken theirs and then grabbed a handful, eating it with relish. Sophia nodded at him as Santa's voice boomed out, "Are you ready for more riddles?"

"Yayyyyyy!" The children clapped encouraging Gino to do a little jig.

"What kinda laundry detergent does Mrs. Santa use? What? No one can guess? Dee ansa is Yule Tide."

The little ones shook their heads and the adults groaned.

"Okay, maybe dat's a bit too hard. Here's an easy one. What does a snowman get when he scratches his head?"

"Snow flakes," the kids yelled.

"Very good. And where does a snowman keep his money?"

"In a snow bank!" the nurses called out. Some of the littlest ones were rolling on the floor laughing out loud.

"What do snowmen eat for breakfast?"

When no one seemed to know the answer, the teenager whispered to the children around him and they screamed, "Frosted flakes!"

Sophia smiled at the boy.

"Here's a tough one. Whatdya call a snowman wearin earmuffs?"

They all looked at each other and then to the nurses for help with the answer. Everyone was stumped.

"You can call him anythin you want cuz he can't hear ya!" Gino proclaimed proudly causing the adults to laugh out loud. "Okay, so enough wid da riddles. I got a story I'd like to tell youse about a little kitten named ZuZu who needs ta find Santa ta make a special wish."

He took out a dog-eared book he'd placed in his sack before he'd left home. ZuZu's Homecoming. He held up the cover showing a sad little kitten all alone under a Christmas tree looking out a window onto a snowstorm and began the tale as the children gathered around listening attentively.

The boy helped bring the wheelchairs closer and sat on the floor between them. Sophia went into the nurse's office to call Kara.

The wind had kept up its howling throughout the late hours of the afternoon into the evening although the snowfall had dwindled. Sergeant Shwinnard came on duty and brought them dinner - big thick turkey sandwiches layered with lettuce, tomato and cheese slathered with his wife's home-made mayonnaise. "I baked my famous Chewy Noels before we lost our electricity," he said putting the picnic basket on a chair since all of the other surfaces were covered with paper. "Why don't you two grab a break and Detective Brown and I can take over for a while. While you're eating, you can bring me up to date on what you've done today."

"I've gone over the evidence we've accumulated during the past week and we decided to get to the bottom of Harknettal and Pruitt's past relationship. We both feel there's too much overlap in their education and job experiences for coincidence."

"I put a call in to some of the people from Louisville and it appears Harknettal obtained his certificate under questionable circumstances. Another Rhode Island administrator Harknettal knew from his time at URI was hired by Louisville. Alan Ordaway, my blogger friend, confirmed there's an ongoing investigation into questions that this guy was taking bribes to falsify some of his cronies' coursework in a program he was running. I'd noticed a discrepancy on Harknettal's resume as to the amount of class work completed before the certificate was granted."

"You think Pruitt was aware of this?" Shwinnard asked.

"Yes, Pruitt spent time at Louisville and he knew the program director from his time in Rhode Island."

"Pruitt may have been using this along with what happened in Cape Cod to blackmail Harknettal."

"I had a relative do some investigating and the school system where they were employed was involved in a scandal. A male phys ed teacher had molested a female student and the parents pressed charges which were later dropped. It appears a monetary settlement with a no disparagement clause was given the family to close the case."

"Was it Pruitt?"

"No, but there was an attempt to cover-up the situation and Harknettal was at the bottom of it. The student was enrolled in special education classes and one of her teachers had reported the allegations to the director who, apparently did no follow-up."

"That would have been Harknettal," Shwinnard said.

"It was. He soon left for the job at Mercy Brown. He was given glowing references. But that's not unusual when a system wants to get rid of a bad apple without their dirty laundry getting dragged out in public," Sullivan informed him.

"So you think Pruitt was using his knowledge of the situations to blackmail Harknettal?"

"I think he followed Harknettal down to Louisville." Using his information from the previous school district, Pruitt made some kind of arrangement to get into the program for an administrator's certificate without doing the work involved," Kara said. "I have people at the college pursuing the matter."

"Did you two find anything else I should be aware of?"

"I keep looking through this folder Pruitt hid at Vida's. It holds resumes with dates underlined and question marks and exclamation points in the margins. But something is missing. I know it."

"What do you mean?" Sullivan asked.

"As we look into all of this, it occurs to me Harknettal paid off Pruitt by fixing up the administration degree and hiring him at the high school. And he tried to get him a raise by taking money from Rosa Brook's salary. There has to be something else Pruitt dug up, probably recently, to continue to have a hold on Harknettal, but it's not in this folder."

"Could he have taken it out of the envelope in the apartment? Maybe it's blowing around town or at the bottom of the Saugatucket? Maybe we'll never find it."

Kara's phone rang and she answered it. "I'll be right over. Thanks, Sophia."

"Is everything okay at the hospital?"

"Beatrice is still holding on but Sophia said that Buddy is in the hospital. He's been helping entertain the kids on the children's ward. I'd like to talk with him if you can arrange a ride for me." She looked outside as the snow continued to fall in the darkness."

"I think we can take care of that request, Detective," Shwinnard picked up the phone. "One snow plow coming up!"

15

MARY, DID YOU KNOW?

They were preparing the children for bedtime. All of them wanted Santa to tuck them in and Gino was making the rounds. Sophia met Kara at the elevator and they rode up together.

"I had them set out a cot in the room for him. He must be exhausted. He's been helping us all afternoon with a few breaks to come up here. I knew who he was immediately, from your description. Did you realize what a kind boy he is?"

"I know. I called his aunt to tell her he was safe with us. From what she told me, he's been watching over his mother for a long time. I need to talk to him," Kara said.

"Are you sure you really want to delve into this? You may not like what you find."

"I have to, Sophia. For my own piece of mind."

"If you decide to stay, I can arrange for a bed. Gino and I are sleeping over tonight."

"I'm just going to sit here and talk with Beatrice," she said and her friend gave her a hug before leaving.

When they were alone, Kara took the frail hand into hers. "Beatrice. It's Detective Langley. Kara. Buddy's going to come by soon. He's been helping to take care of the children today. It's been snowing for hours and their parents can't get in to see them. Wires are down and keeping the roads plowed has been almost impossible, what with the strong winds and the drifts. But you're safe inside and it's warm. Kara smoothed the blanket. I'll let you rest." She sat back in the chair and waited.

The boy entered the room and stood by her chair looking down at his mother.

"Hello, Buddy."

"Hello, Detective Langley." He glanced at the cot. "The nurses thought you might want to stay here tonight."

He pulled a chair around to the other side of the bed and sat very straight.

"Do you think my mother's going to be all right?" He looked into Kara's eyes.

"I don't know," Kara answered him truthfully.

"I wish there was something I could do to help her," he said.

"I think just sitting by her side and being here is the best thing you can do right now. I've been talking to her and I told her you'd be coming to visit."

He leaned over and whispered, "Hi, Mama. It's me Buddy. Don't worry, I've been taking care of the house for you. I'm right here. I won't leave you. I promise." He tucked the doll in closer to her.

"Did you bring that to her?"

"Yes, it was a gift from my father. She loved dolls and she saw that one in the window of a toy store when they were dating. My dad wrapped it up and put it under the Christmas tree that year. He told her no one was ever too old to get a toy for Christmas."

"Mrs. Carnivale said you helped with the children today. The nurses were glad to have the help."

"It must be hard for the little guys to be in the hospital and not to see their parents."

"Sometimes other people have to step in when a parent isn't able. You made those children very happy today, Buddy."

"It was fun. It made me feel like a kid again."

"But you are ..." Kara didn't finish the sentence.

"Detective Langley, that night ... I heard the doctor say you found her lying in the snow. Do you know why she did it?" Again he looked into her eyes and again she answered truthfully.

"I don't know, Buddy."

"My mom's been sad for a long time. I used to hate her for what she'd done. I blamed her," he said. "But I know she couldn't help it. Now, I just feel so sorry for her."

Kara nodded her head. She found she had no voice. This conversation was breaking her heart. They sat in silence.

He began to nod off and went to the cot. "I'm going to lie down for a few minutes."

The wind had abated and gentle flakes fluttered outside the window. Kara felt fingertips gently touching her wrist.

"Detective Langley?"

"Yes, Beatrice."

"Why?" She looked imploringly at Kara. "I wanted to die."

"I'll get the nurse for you."

"Wait! The note?"

"I have it here." She took it from her pocket.

"I killed Sherman."

"I don't believe you did."

"Please. Do you have children?" She clutched Kara's hand.

Kara hesitated and then confided in her, "I'm expecting my first child in the spring."

"Wonderful news!" She stopped talking until she'd regained some strength. "I've been a terrible mother," Beatrice gasped for breath. "Couldn't take care of my own child."

"Mama?" The two women looked at the boy standing at the end of the hospital bed.

Kara got up from the chair, "Buddy, come sit down."

She left him holding his mother's hand. Taking her coat, she went to tell the nurse that Mrs. Pruitt was awake and then she called for Stewart to come and bring her home.

Saturday, December 9

16

OH, TIDINGS OF COMFORT AND JOY

The town had spent the last two days digging out from the storm. Snowdrifts were as high as three story buildings. The good news was that most of the power had been restored and people began coming out of their houses to resume activities temporarily halted by the weather.

Kara and Stewart were spending the morning in town shopping for the party they were hosting on Sunday. "I think it's time to break the news to our friends. Sophia keeps giving me sly looks and making comments that lead me to believe she's already guessed."

"She's probably known since the moment of conception," Stewart said making them both laugh as they walked around Belmont's putting groceries into their basket.

"I was hoping to wait until after the wedding, but I think this will work out well," she said.

"When we get home, we should call our families. I don't know who's going to be more excited, your brother or my sister." He stopped halfway down the condiments aisle to examine the pickle varieties. "So, do you have any cravings?"

"Not really. I'm finding a slight aversion to coffee and runny eggs."

"What about cucumbers, pistachio ice cream, lime Jell-O, avocados, honeydew melon, split pea soup?"

"Runny eggs and anything green," she added as she quickly steered the cart away from the guacamole and green onion dip.

They rounded the corner just as a little boy came rushing toward them. He climbed underneath their cart. Billy Sullivan was in hot pursuit of his brother, followed by his mother.

"Connor, get out from under there!" Billy warned. He tried to get hold of one foot in an attempt to help his mother who was busy making sure Connor didn't bang his head. He ended up with a tiny shoe in his hand.

"Sorry about this." Jess stood up to move to the other side of the basket. The older boy ran to retrieve their groceries. "Oh, hi, Dr. Langley. Kara."

Billy returned with a big chocolate and marshmallow Santa Claus. He held it out to the two-year-old and just as Connor lunged at it, his mother gathered him up and swiftly set him back in the cart seat, firmly strapping him in.

"It's good to see you both. And I want to thank you again for volunteering to babysit next Friday night," she said to Kara as she headed toward the checkout.

Kara put her hand on her stomach and looked at her husband. "What were we possibly thinking?"

"About babysitting or the decision to start a family?" he asked.

They turned and watched as the little boy began climbing onto the conveyor belt with the groceries.

"Both!" She answered.

Vida hadn't taken a shower in days. No electricity meant no pump and it didn't look like she was going to get water back any time soon. Her area was remote and not heavily populated. It was one of the last neighborhoods in the town to be taken care of, but she was used to this. She decided to treat herself to a spa day and used the last of her cell phone charge to book an appointment in Wakefield. The woman who answered the phone informed her they'd had lots of cancellations and she could come in any time.

"I'd like to git my hair done and styled and a mani-pedi and one of those hot rocks massage … I'm thinkin I'd like a festive look … Nope, I think I'll stay away from the red and green motif and go more for purple and maroon. Maybe a little tangerine thrown in? Can you do that? All rightee then! See you in a bit … And I gotta warn ya - I stink!"

After she signed into the spa , she went to the women's area to take a long hot shower and then sit in the hot tub. Only one other person was in the garden room and she stepped into the tub, settling in directly across from Vida.

"Hey! You look familiar. What's your name?"

The young woman hesitated before answering. "Loralei."

"Nice name. I'm Vida. Where do I know you from?" Vida asked.

"I work here on Saturdays. Right now I'm on my lunch break. Have you come in before?"

"This is my first time."

"I have a night job in Wakefield at the Glassworks Shop. Have you ever been in the studio?"

"Can't say that I have. But I know the place. It's on the corner of Robinson and Main. I'm not much for knick knacks and the stuff in your store is real expensive."

"It's hand blown. We give demonstrations."

Vida snapped her fingers. "I rememba where I seen you. You were at Sherm's memorial service the other day."

"I work part time at Kenyon Florists. I delivered the floral arrangements."

"You were sittin in the back row," Vida persisted. "Did you know Sherm?"

"Not well. He was the vice principal at my school. But I know Buddy."

"His stepson?"

"Yes, Buddy Tetreault. I hadn't realize they were related until Saturday. Buddy never told me his stepdad's name. He stops by the glass shop every night around ten to say 'Hi' and see if I'm okay."

"What are you doin alone in a shop at ten at night?"

"I like to work on my own and it's quiet. Nobody coming in and out to bother me. I have to concentrate. The fire is intense and the molten glass can do a number on your skin if you're not paying attention." She slid closer to show Vida the burn scars on her wrists and arms.

"Ouch!" That must've hurt. "You could get some tatoos to cover those up." Vida picked up her feet to show off her art work.

"That's real nice," the girl agreed, "but I'm terrified of needles."

"That's okay. We all got our phobias," Vida said. "So, you know Buddy? He's a nice kid."

"I used to be afraid of him at first. I'd see him walking around the village late at night and I made sure the door was locked. But one night, I saw him watching me mold the glass with the rods and he was smiling like a little kid. I asked if he'd like to come in and I explained the whole process. He was full of questions. And every night after that, if he saw me in the shop, he'd stop and wave and give me a peace sign."

"What was he doing out on the streets at that time of night?"

"He lives with his aunt, you know, but he told me he kept a check on his mother, to make sure she was safe. He said he was worried about her. She sometimes roams and she has blackouts. Because of the drinking."

"Ya know his mom's in the hospital?"

"No. That's too bad. I didn't have a chance to talk with him on Saturday. I had another delivery, so I left the service before it ended."

"What did you talk about when he came by the shop?"

"Mostly about school and music. He's in the band. I was in the band at my school before I quit last week."

"You quit? Me, too. And I've always been sorry. Some day I'm gonna git my GED and then I might just go on to take some college classes," Vida told the girl. "Why'd you quit?"

"I turned eighteen and my mom's boyfriend said it was time I went out on my own."

"And your mom was okay with that?"

"She's not a very strong person. She hates confrontations. I wanted to get out of the house, anyway. I make pretty good money with all my jobs. I'll miss school, though. Even with my jobs, I got straight A's and I only had one semester left."

"I left school when I turned sixteen. Wish I'd stuck it out, but we needed the money," Vida told the girl.

"I found out I can get into community college without a diploma," Loralei said.

"You can do that?"

"I'm planning on it. I work here on Saturdays and I put the whole paycheck into a college fund. I'll probably have to use some of it as a damage deposit when I find a place to live, but I think my other jobs might cover expenses."

"I got a spare room and you're welcome to stay. I won't charge you nothin. You just gotta help me study for my GED."

The girl began to cry.

"Oh, dangit! Loralei, what did I say? I'm always sayin the wrong things!"

The girl shook her head. "You're being so kind and you don't even know me."

"Look, you'll be doing me a favor. I got a spare room to rent and you can help me check one of the goals off my bucket list."

"I'll think about it. I have to get back to work."

"I'll be here all day. I'll write out directions to my place for you. You can move in as soon as you want. The room's all cleaned out. Just gotta turn the mattress."

"Thanks, Vida. I've been worried – not even sure where I was going to be this Christmas. You've made me feel so much better."

"We can all use a little bit of help every now and then. I wish someone had been there for me when I was your age. I might have become a different person."

"But then, you wouldn't be you and I think you're wonderful just the way you are, Vida."

"The tuba section is getting better but I don't think it will be our best concert ever," he confided in his aunt and stepsister.

"Miracles can happen, Buddy." Evelyn told him.

"I know. My mom is awake. She even let me feed her some baby food last night!"

After Buddy left with his friends, Suzanne phoned the hospital and was told family could visit but couldn't stay too long.

"I think it would be okay if we paid her a visit. She'll be so happy to see you Evie," Suzanne said. "I'm going to bring some cookies for the nurses."

"I'll drive. The sidewalks are too slippery for us to walk up the hill."

"And we can do some shopping afterwards," Suzy suggested.

Beatrice was waiting for them. The nurse had told her she was going to have visitors and they dressed her in her new pink plush robe, open so the top of her fleece nightgown with its candy cane design could be seen. The red slippers were on the floor by the side of the bed.

"Don't you look festive, Bea!" Suzanne kissed her forehead. "Look who came to see you."

Evelyn stepped forward, trying to keep the shock at the drastic change in her stepmother from registering on her face. "Hi, Mom. I'm so glad to see you." Bea grabbed her hand, squeezing it weakly.

They positioned themselves on either side of the bed. "We can't stay long. The nurses don't want you to get too tired. I spoke with Ed this morning and told him I'd call when I got home from seeing you."

"He's a good friend," Bea told them. She took a deep breath of oxygen from the plastic tubes inserted in her nose. "I have to ask you to help me."

"Of course, Bea. That's what family is for. You can stay with me as long as you want when they release you from the hospital," Suzanne told her.

"I'm not going to leave here." She began to cry as she looked beseechingly at her sister-in-law.

"Of course you are Mom," Evelyn comforted her.

Bea patted her step-daughter's hand. "Evie, could you ask the nurse at the desk if I could have some juice?"

"Sure. I'll be right back."

"Buddy will always be taken care of, Bea. Please don't worry," Suzy continued.

"Buddy's glove. I took it the night I came by to tell you about Sherm."

"The orange glove?"

"Yes." She stopped to breathe in the oxygen. "The other one was found in the store. I took it from the reshelving bin the next day when I realized it was his. I'm sure Detective Langley knows about the glove and she suspects he was there that night." She closed her eyes. "Suzy, you have to tell them he was with you. That he never left the apartment."

"But, how did ..."

Beatrice interrupted Suzy. "I'm confessing to the murder. I wrote a note. Detective Langley has it but she hasn't turned it in. I'm going to tell the police myself when they interview me."

"Did you do it, Bea? Did you murder Sherm?" Suzy looked into her eyes.

"I don't know. I can't remember anything about Thanksgiving night. I think I was at the store and Buddy walked me home. I remember him putting the covers over me."

"But it could have been a dream, Bea," Suzy's voice caught in her throat and she sat processing what she'd just heard when Evelyn returned.

"There were a few choices, so I brought you one of each. Apple, orange or cranberry." Evelyn put the containers on the table.

"Apple, please," Bea looked nervously at Suzy as she sipped the juice from the straw and then rested her head back onto the pillow. Suzy nodded.

A nurse came in to give Beatrice a shot. "Mrs. Pruitt's going to need her rest. You can come back to see her tomorrow."

Evelyn and Suzy said their goodbyes and left the hospital.

"I'm glad I got to visit her," Evelyn said. "Maybe we can talk a little more before I leave for Maine?"

Suzanne didn't answer.

"Suzy, are you okay?"

"Yes, I'm fine. Just a little shocked at how frail she is."

"Do you still want to go shopping?" Evelyn asked.

"Yes, I need to buy a pair of gloves."

Sunday, December 10

17

Yeah, It Would Have Been Different Back Then, If There Were Three Wise Women Not Three Wise Men

Suzanne listened to the priest as he explained the four traditional Advent themes, one for each Sunday - Hope, Peace, Love, Joy. And the fifth candle representing the birth of Christ. Her mind wandered in and out of the sermon. It was difficult to concentrate, so much had been filling her head since she'd spoken with Beatrice. She had always considered herself an honest person – to a fault. But that had changed since Thanksgiving. She touched Buddy's hand on her left and then Evelyn's on her right.

Evie would be leaving for Maine today. She was going to miss her. Another woman in the house to talk with. But she and Beatrice could not share what they knew with her even though Evelyn would do anything to protect Buddy. The three of them would do anything.

"On the second Sunday in Advent, the Candle of Peace is lit like a light shining in a dark place," Father Langevin explained from the pulpit. Suzanne needed to seek peace. She was in a dark place. Beatrice was not doing well. She'd had a relapse and the doctors were cautiously monitoring her liver functions and her heart. They called from the hospital just before the family left for church.

She decided not to tell Buddy and Evie. They would attend Mass and then have a special dinner before sending Evie home. She'd explain the situation when they spoke on Monday. Later in the evening, she and Buddy would go to the hospital.

Before Mass she had taken Father Langevin aside and asked if he would visit Beatrice and hear her confession. He assured her he'd be at the hospital directly after service.

"Love is like a candle helping guide us through all the troubles of this world," the priest told them.

Suzanne closed her eyes and said a prayer for Beatrice, for Buddy and for herself.

Rosa Brooks was pouring a second cup of coffee when the phone rang. "Hello ... Vida ... of course I remember you ... You did? ... I'm not very busy at the moment. You live nearby so I could come and pick it up, if that's convenient ... I recognize the street. Sherm's old address. I'll be there in fifteen minutes."

Vida and Loralei had been turning the mattress over on the bed when Loralei noticed an envelope poking from a rip in the box springs. She inched it out and read the label on the outside. "School Funds". "Should we open it to see what's inside?"

"No, I'm gonna call Ms. Brooks. She'll know what to do."

"Good idea. I really liked her. She's a wonderful principal. And fair. She treated the poorer kids the same as the ones who had money or played sports. When I called to tell her I wouldn't be coming back to school, I think it really bothered her. She tried to talk me out of it."

They moved the mattress back into place and began to make up the bed with fresh linens. "Look, I bought pillowcases with candies on them. Sugarplums, the lady in the store called them. It reminded me of "The Night before Christmas", Vida said.

"And visions of sugarplums danced in their heads," they recited together.

"I think it means children were having sweet dreams," Loralei said.

"I like that idea. We could all use some sweet dreams around here. Well, you just unpack and git settled in. I'm gonna make some hot chocolate for when Ms. Brooks gits here," Vida announced.

Rosa had barely rapped on the door before it was opened. "Cmon in. It's nice to see you agin. This time there's no dead body and the music is a lot cheerier. Gimme yer coat. I'll just hang it up ... Loralei!

Ms. Brooks is here." The girl came from the bedroom into the living room.

"Loralei, what a nice surprise. I missed you this week. I called your mother, but she didn't know where you'd gone."

"Actually, I've just moved in here this morning. Vida had a spare room to rent and I had nowhere to go."

"I'm so relieved you're safe. You should call your mom and tell her where you are."

"I planned on doing that as soon as I unpacked my stuff."

"And we need to discuss you finishing your last semester. You've only missed a week and with your grades, catching up shouldn't be a problem."

"I have to work. I can't just freeload. And I need to save up for college."

"I'm sure the three of us can put our heads together and reach a solution you can live with. If you haven't realized it yet, Vida is a force of nature. And I believe she'll want to do what's best for you. I know I do."

Vida returned with a tray of cocoa and cookies shaped like little reindeer heads. "It's nice to have company on a Sunday afternoon. This'll be like those ladies' teas they have in England." She poured cocoa from a large white teapot decorated with a jolly Mrs. Claus who was serving tea around a table to a group of lady elves. The china cups and saucers had a holly design around the rim. "Hava cookie. I made'em myself this mornin'. The recipe was on a bag of chocolate kisses."

"This is lovely Vida."

"Thanks, I usually use a mug, but the ones I got are all chipped. The saucers are more fancy, although ya don't get as much cocoa in em."

"A cup is plenty for me. I'm curious. You said you had something I'd be interested in. Something that was in Sherm's possession."

"Loralei found it hidden in the box spring when we were gittin the room ready for her to move in." Vida handed the envelope to Rosa. The flap was sealed with silver duct tape.

177

"School funds?" Rosa pulled the tape off ripping the envelope. Money and a key spilled on to the floor.

"Whoa! That's a lotta moola," Vida helped gather it up. She and Evelyn counted the bills.

Rosa read the paperwork contained in the envelope with the money. "It looks like Sherman had a special account he'd opened up years ago when he worked at the Cape. And the co-signer was Superintendent Harknettal. I think we need to show this to Detective Sullivan. It could be tied in with their deaths."

"The party was in full swing. Vince Guaraldi's Christmas album was playing and Gino was in his Santa outfit demonstrating how to dance like Charley Brown and his Peanuts gang.

"Should he be bouncing up and down like that? He's had a lot of beer and that suit doesn't look easy to get out of fast," Kara asked.

"He's got a bladder like a giant sponge," Sophia assured her.

"Good to know!"

"Clay must wonder if he's ever getting his costume back," Ruth said.

"That suit's going to need a good cleaning. He almost never takes it off."

Sophia reached for her empty wine glass and said to Stewart, "Hit me again!"

"I was wondering if he wears it to bed," Rick commented out loud. Sophia gave him a nasty look and he quickly added "Well, not the boots, obviously. That could hurt."

"I would change the topic if I were you. It's becoming a bone of contention with them," Kara warned Rick as his sister-in-law began to get up from her chair to move in closer to him.

"How 'bout those Pats!" He declared loudly to a room full of people not the least bit interested in the New England Patriots or football in general. Sophia did not look appeased.

"Maybe you should come help me in the kitchen?" Stewart suggested, guiding Rick safely out of the living room.

With the men engrossed in other activities, the three friends sat talking about the wedding. "Everything is done. I finished the alter-atiions on Kara's dress. Hopefully we won't have to let it out any more before Christmas," Sophia gave Kara her squinty-eyed stare.

"Kara cleared her throat and called into the kitchen. "Guys, would you come back in here for a moment please? Gino, could you dance over here? We have something to share with you."

Stewart turned the music down and put his arm around his wife as their friends gathered round. "We're expecting a baby in the spring-time," he announced.

Hugs and congratulations followed with toasts to the parents-to-be.

"We were going to wait until after the wedding. We didn't want to take anything away from your special day. But I'm not sure either of us could keep it a secret for much longer," Kara explained.

Rick gave Ruth a napkin to wipe the tears from her face.

"This is wonderful news. We need to start shopping for maternity clothes and of course there'll be the baby shower to plan. I'll need to start keeping notes," Sophia said.

Stewart went into the den and came back with an extra large loose-leaf binder for her. "We thought you could use this."

Gino turned up the music and grabbed Kara's arm and spun her around in the middle of the floor. He pointed to his wife. "Sophia, you was right! A liddle baby. In da springtime. Now, dat's somethin ta dance about!"

Detective Brown and Sergeant Shwinnard searched the house for anything Sherman may have hidden. They discovered a strong box hidden under the attic floorboards. Sullivan and Carlyle did a thorough check of Pruitt's bedroom and other places downstairs but found nothing else. Brown crawled into the space beneath the house and came out with another metal container. The key inside the envelope opened the boxes to reveal more money and a letter signed by Sherman Pruitt.

If you find this letter and I have died under
questionable circumstances, look to Superinten-
dent Hyram Harknettal as a prime suspect. Hyram
and I were involved in various financial dealings
in the districts where we worked together. I have
written a detailed explanation of our business
ventures and proof that Hyram first involved me
in his plans when I was employed as a janitor in
the Old Rockingham School System and subsequently
coerced me to be complicit in schemes within the
other districts where we worked.
(A key to a safety deposit box at the Washing-
ton Trust Bank in Wakefield is on a key ring in
Beatrice Pruitt's possession. She has no idea
that I did this.)
Sherman L. Pruitt

After all of the evidence had been collected, Sullivan thanked the three women for their help. "I'll make sure any funds belonging to your school will be returned to you, Ms. Brooks. It appears, from this paperwork, Sherman kept detailed records."

"I'm not surprised about that one bit," Vida said. The guy was a slob, but one thing he was meticulous about was money."

"All right, excitement's over. How about we continue with our Lady's Tea and put our three heads together to come up with a plan to get you back to school?" She put her arm around Loralei and they followed Vida back into the house.

Sullivan phoned Kara to tell her about his afternoon. "Tomorrow I'm going to be speaking with Beatrice. We could have this case wrapped up by the end of the week. Looks like you were absolutely right about not jumping to make an arrest before all the facts were in. Thanks for your help with this. I could have made a big mistake if it weren't for your advice." His voice sounded relieved.

"You're welcome. We all make mistakes sometime. I'll see you in the morning."

She took the note from her pocket and unfolded it, silently reading Beatrice Pruitt's confession. Then she folded it and put it into her desk ddrawer.

Later in the evening, Sophia called the hospital to check on Beatrice. She relayed the information to Kara. "Beatrice has relapsed."

"Detective Sullivan intended to question her tomorrow."

"I don't expect that's going to happen, now. She's very weak. Suzanne and Buddy were with her and the priest gave her the Last Rites."

"I'd like to see her one more time," Kara said.

"Good news amidst sad." Sophia gave Kara a kiss. "We're all so happy for you and Stewart. Take care of yourself. This baby is important to all of us, you know. Get some rest while you can. In a few months you'll be a new mom and look back on this time in a fog of exhaustion."

After Stewart and Kara had said goodbye to their friends, they sat discussing the day and sipping tea in front of the fireplace.

"Well, that went well," Kara said.

"When do you think Sophia guessed?"

"She'd been making sly comments ever since we returned from our trip out to see the solar eclipse last August," Kara chuckled.

"Why don't you sit here and rest and I'll finish straightening up the kitchen?" Stewart suggested.

"I'd like to visit Beatrice. Sophia thinks she's failing quickly and I'm afraid she could be right. I just need to speak with her one last time."

"It's getting late. Do you want me to go with you to the hospital?"

"No, I'm not going to stay long. I'll be home before you finish drying the dishes."

She settled into the chair and looked sadly at the woman in the bed. She held her frail hand.

"Hello, Beatrice. It's Kara. I've been thinking a lot about what you said. I'm not sure exactly what it means to be a good mother. I guess I'll just have to learn on the job. Like learning how to be a good cop. I'm afraid I'll make some mistakes. Hopefully, I'll avoid most. I'll try to listen to people who are wiser than me. Who've had more experience. It's too bad we have to make mistakes to get experience, though.

"Detective Sullivan found evidence today that points to someone else for Sherman's death. You know I never believed you could kill anyone unless it was to protect your son. I thought it might be the case that you and Buddy were there that night. You could have stabbed Sherman if he was hurting Buddy. You'd done it before. Or Buddy could have stabbed his stepfather while Sherm was attacking you. I'm not sure and now I guess I'll never know. In the end, I'd rather believe that your abusive husband was murdered by his odious partner in crime and that justice was done.

"I really want the world I bring my child into to be like that. And we both know if she's a girl, she's going to have some serious hills to climb. But I'm going to surround her with as many loving people as I can. You entrusted your son to the person you knew would love him as much as you did. It must have been hard to give him up. You did your best to protect him and I want you to know that I'll be there for him, too."

She clasped the pale white hand in hers. "Beatrice, you are a good mother. Don't ever doubt you did the right thing for your son. He's a caring young man. You and Suzy should be proud."

She placed Beatrice's hand underneath the covers. On the cot in the corner of the room, the boy stirred and as Kara left the room she heard him whisper, "Thank you."

Tuesday, December 12

18

If Only in My Dreams

On Tuesday morning, Carl Sullivan met with Mrs. Harknettal to go over her final statement. She'd lied to him the first time he'd questioned her and he'd given her the chance to rectify the situation and not have charges brought against her.

"You said your husband had a temper and you feared he would hurt you if you didn't give him an alibi for the night Sherman Pruitt was killed. Is that true, Mrs. Harknettal?"

"Yes, Hyram was prone to violence when he didn't get his way."

"On the night of November 23rd, when did you last see your husband?"

"We'd had dinner and I was cleaning up around seven thirty, when the doorbell rang. Hyram answered it and I could hear someone arguing with him. I looked in to see if everything was okay and Hyram told me to mind my own business."

"Who was with your husband?"

"Sherman Pruitt. He'd obviously been drinking and was slurring his words."

"What were they arguing about?"

"Sherman was angry with my husband about being fired. He asked Hyram who he was going to get to replace him and cover for his sorry ass. Hyram tried to calm him down by reasoning with him. He reminded Sherman he was arranging for a job in another district."

"And did he calm down?"

"His voice got lower but it seemed to be even more threatening. He told my husband it would be a cold day in hell before he worked with another woman and he could shove his reference for that two bit district Hyram had arranged for him to be assigned."

"How did Hyram react?"

"Hyram tried to mollify him. He said if he didn't like the new job, he could take his share of the money and buy that dream home in Florida he was always talking about. Sherman was furious. He told Hyram he was going to take his share all right. He was going to take both their shares and warned my husband not to try to stop him because he had lots of information that could ruin him and he wouldn't hesitate to use it. Then he left. Hyram grabbed his coat and ran out to the car and drove down the street after him."

"Did he tell you where he was going?"

"No."

"When did he arrive home?"

"I'm a light sleeper. I heard the car in the driveway and looked at my cell phone on the night table. It was eleven twenty-three. I thought I heard him doing a laundry but maybe I was dreaming. Hyram never did housework."

"What time did he go to bed?"

"I'm not sure. We have separate bedrooms. I fell asleep but I woke up for a few seconds when heard a door slam."

"Thank you for your cooperation, Mrs. Harknettal. You're free to go."

"I'm not in trouble for what I told you last week?"

"No, this will be your official statement."

"Thank you, Detective Sullivan. You've been more than kind to give me another chance."

For the remainder of the morning Sullivan and his team went over the paperwork they'd retrieved from the safe deposit box. Sergeant Shwinnard took out his notes to read with Sullivan and Brown.

"Harknettal and Pruitt had accumulated a small fortune in the years they'd been devising ways to move money from the schools into their own pockets. Cash from fundraisers, bribes, slush funds, and kickbacks from construction contracts. The two of them had found every manner of syphoning school funds into their account. Statements and copies of records found in the safe deposit box indicated Harknettal had taken the larger share over the years. It explained his Italian designer suits and handcrafted leather shoes, his German sports car, the addition of a video room to his house."

Detective Brown had discovered further incriminating evidence. "I looked into one of Pruitt's most lucrative schemes which involved ordering the supplies for vending machines in bulk, storing them and loading the machines himself leaving out the middle man. He kept the keys to all the machines and collected the money after school each day. Unlike the other scams, it provided a regular steady stream of cash. A recent letter from Harknettal warned Pruitt he'd found out about it and expected to receive his cut. A copy of a letter from Pruitt to Harknettal threatened to expose the fact that the superintendent's certificate was invalid. Their longstanding complicity obviously had begun to crumble under the weight of the increasing problems Pruitt was having at school when Ms. Brooks began looking into harassment complaints."

"It appeared she was not letting Sherman get away with much and he was becoming frustrated. He wanted her fired," Sullivan added."

Detective Brown jumped in. "That's correct. A forensics check on Harknettal's computer provided even more information into their ongoing schemes. An email from Pruitt to Harknettal outlined methods he was using to undermine Ms. Brooks in the hope of getting rid of her. Harknettal's response was to encourage him and offer him more pay if he could accomplish his goal."

"If Pruitt had just behaved for a short time, he probably would have been made principal after Harknettal had figured a way to get Brooks fired," he said. The phone rang and Sullivan took the call.

"Hey, congratulations, Lieutenant! Welcome to the wonderful world of parenting. At least you've got a few months of peace left to enjoy."

"Wow, news travels fast," Kara marveled.

"Ruth told Arthur who told Leo who told everyone here at the station. Who needs social media in this town?"

"I'm surprised Kendra Gravelle hasn't already published an article on the impending birth for Friday's edition of The Narragansett Times."

"She called this morning looking to see if I had the report on the results of the Pruitt and Harknettal investigations so she could finish writing her story. We're working on it now. I told her it wouldn't be completed until later in the week but gave her the scoop on the future Langley baby," he teased. "You and Stewart could make this week's front page."

"I wish I could believe you're just kidding. So, how is the report coming along?"

"I'd like you to look at the final draft over before I turn it in - to make sure the case we're building doesn't have any gaps. I've been working on the motivation for Harknettal killing Pruitt. Sergeant Brown took the photo of Harknettal's flashy sports car around the village. The manager at Healy's remembered it parked across the street in front of the old post office building a little before ten when he started to close up for the night."

"So, he has motive and you can place him at the scene. Good job."

"And Harknettal's death is looking more like an accident. His blood alcohol level was high and he could have stumbled against the railing. No marks on his body, but he was wearing two pillows, so he was well padded. I'd like to know your thoughts on it."

"I plan on stopping to see Suzanne Tetreault today. She called me last night to tell me Beatrice is not doing well."

"Thanks, again, for not letting me charge Beatrice for her husband's murder. That would have been a big mistake."

Suzanne had left the front door ajar and was sitting on the couch when Kara arrived.

"Just hang up your coat in the hall," she called out.

On the ledge above the hook was a pair of orange gloves, just like the ones Beatrice was wearing the night Kara found her at the church. And exactly like the one she'd taken a photo of the day the body was found in the dressing room at Kenyon's. She wondered if the two women had worked out a plan?

She was sure Beatrice had removed the glove from the bin of items to be shelved. It wasn't there on Tuesday when Kara visited the store. Everything else in the photo was still in the bin, but not the glove. She knew it was Buddy's. The scarf he wore was an exact match. And the color of the clothes in Beatrice's closet and drawers, except for the white underwear, were blacks and beiges and the gloves in her closet were gray Isotoners. Her winter coat was white. She certainly wasn't one to sport a pair of orange gloves like the ones Kara had examined and placed in storage at the forensics lab. They were definitely Buddy's which meant he was at Kenyon's the night of his stepfather's murder.

Even if Beatrice had been there herself and had a blackout, seeing the glove in the bin would have signaled to her that her son was at the store that night.

When they'd searched Suzanne's apartment after the break-in, she'd noticed no orange gloves. But here they were in plain view in the hall with the matching scarf. Like his mother, Suzanne was ensuring that he couldn't be placed at the scene of Sherman's murder. She wondered what story they worked out regarding the circumstances surrounding Harknettal's death.

Kara envisioned Buddy coming home to find a stranger in the house and chasing him out the back door. They struggled on the bridge and Harknettal fell into the river. The boy probably stood frozen on the bridge, afraid of the water and unable to save the man drowning in the river beneath him.

The only evidence she had that someone from the house had been at the scene and retrieved the stolen papers was the dampness of the envelope. And Suzanne could explain that away because it was next to the sink. Even if they could put someone on the bridge struggling with Harknettal that night, Kara was sure Suzanne would confess to chasing the intruder from the house before letting Buddy admit to it. Kara entered the apartment.

"Hello, Suzanne. How are you and Buddy doing?"

"He seems to be better since Father Langevin gave Bea the Last Rites. He decided not to stay with her last night. He'll go after school today for a few hours. He's resigned she won't be getting better - that she won't be home for Christmas."

"He's been through so much. I find Buddy to be extremely wise for someone his age," Kara said.

Suzanne changed the subject. "How's the investigation going?"

"Detective Sullivan is hoping to have it completed and his report in by the end of the week. I'll be working with him this afternoon. We'll make sure you have all the information before it's made public."

"Does he think Hyram Harknettal killed Sherman?"

"It would appear the superintendent had the means, motive and opportunity. Did Beatrice say anything to you about the night of the murder?"

"She was very weak and Evie and I spent most of our time telling her about our Christmas plans. We'd hoped she would be able to celebrate with us. I think she realized it was not to be."

Kara turned to leave. She went into the hall and Suzanne helped her on with her coat.

"You look good in red. It suits you."

When Kara had reached the bottom of the staircase, Suzanne said, "Thank you, Detective Langley. You and Detective Sullivan have been caring and considerate of us during this difficult time."

She waited until Kara was at the bottom of the stairs. "Don't bother to lock the door. My nephew will be home soon. And congratulations. We were talking the other night and Buddy told me he thinks you'll be a great mother."

Thursday, December 14

19

LONG LAY THE WORLD
IN SIN AND ERROR PINING

Outside in the dark hours of Thursday morning, the Geminid Meteor showers were at their height. Streaks of light plummeted from the cloudless skies while in the quiet of the hospital room, with her son by her side, Beatrice Pruitt died.

On the front steps of the hospital, Buddy looked up to make a wish on one of the falling stars. He walked down Kenyon Avenue past his mother's house and stopped to look at the Christmas tree in the window. At the bottom of the hill, the candles in his aunt's apartment let him know she was waiting for him to come home.

When the first of the morning light shone through the lace curtains into the room, Suzanne phoned Kara to tell her Beatrice was finally at peace.

"I wish life could have been different for her, but she never seemed to come out from under the shadow of Daniel's death," Suzanne confided in her.

"How is Buddy?" Kara asked.

"He'd like to speak with you." Suzanne handed him the phone.

"Hello, Detective Langley."

"Buddy, I'm so sorry to hear about your mom."

"Thank you, Detective. I was wondering if we could talk?"

"Of course." She waited for him to continue.

"Not on the phone. I'm going to speak with Father Langevin in an hour or so. We won't be long. Could you meet me at the church?"

"I'll be there, Buddy."

He was sitting up front and looked over his shoulder at the sound of the door opening She walked down the aisle and sat next to him.

"Detective Langley, I want you to know what happened. My aunt is trying to protect me, but now that my mother is gone, there are things I need to tell you. Things you already may have figured out."

"Have you spoken with your aunt about this?"

"I told her I couldn't let her take the blame for what I did. And I talked to my mom. I'm not sure she heard me, but I explained how I couldn't live with the lies. Even though the truth is hard sometimes, lies can eat you up. Father Langevin agrees with me."

"Why don't you share what you know with me and we'll decide what to do next?

"I was there. Thanksgiving night – at the store. When we got home from dinner, I waited until my aunt was asleep and went to check on my mom. Like I did most nights. She wasn't at home and the front door was open. I'd found her wandering around the neighborhood twice before and so I went looking for her. I noticed a light on in her office. The back door was open and she was at her desk. A man's jacket was on the floor. She told me Sherman was drunk. He'd brought her to the store to steal him a leather coat. She grabbed me by the arm, pleading, "You've got to stop him, Buddy. I'll get in big trouble. The file cabinet drawers were open. I closed them and when I turned, she had put her head on the desk and was asleep. I heard noises upstairs. It was pretty dark but the moon gave enough light so I could see two men fighting. One of the men was pushing the other one back over the counter top, choking him. I ran to stop him, but right then, the man who was being attacked grabbed at something next to the register and stabbed the guy who had him by the neck. He fell back and I heard the sound of the mirror cracking."

"What were they fighting about?"

"One of them was calling the other a thief and yelling about a file. The other guy, the killer, couldn't say much. He just grabbed for the spindle and the next thing I knew, I was running down the stairs to wake my mom. I was scared he would hurt her, too. I shook her and got her up. She didn't have a coat, so I put the jacket on her and took her back up to the house and into bed. I locked the doors and waited to see if anyone had followed us."

"And the jacket?"

"When it was light, I started back home. I stopped at the store. It was locked, so I put the jacket in the car parked next to the back door. I didn't know it was my stepfather who was killed until the next day and then I was afraid to get my mother involved. I never reported it. If I had, maybe the other man wouldn't have died."

"That man made some bad choices which led to his death. You couldn't have prevented that."

"I know it was wrong not to call 911 and I'm ready to take the consequences. The worse thing was when I heard my mom and you talking. She thought I did it. She thought I murdered my stepdad. She'd found my glove. I explained to her what happened and I think it eased her mind.'"

"I'm sure it did, Buddy. She loved you very much."

"I know. She was going to take the blame for me. She didn't remember any of that night except me putting her to bed."

"Does your aunt know what happened?"

"I told her this morning when I came home from the hospital. She said I should talk to you," he hesitated for a minute. "And there's something else."

"About the man who drowned?"

"Yes. He was in the apartment when I arrived home. He had Evie's envelope. I chased him outside and caught up to him on the bridge. When I grabbed the envelope, he lost his balance and fell into the river. I couldn't save him. I just stood on the bridge not able to move."

"You're afraid of the water, I know."

"But I should have done something and I didn't. Would you come to the police station with me so I can tell Detective Sullivan the truth? I need to tell him the truth."

"I'm going to call a friend who's a lawyer and then I'll phone your aunt and tell her we'll pick her up on our way to the station. After you give your statement, you'll be placed into her custody and she'll take you home. It's going to be okay," she reassured him.

In a second's time he went from a young adult to looking like a helpless child. "My mother said I could trust you. You'll stay with me? I can't do this alone."

"I won't leave you, Buddy."

"I wanted to tell someone earlier, but I had to take care of her. I thought I could keep her safe. She doesn't need me now."

While Kara made her phone calls, Buddy knelt in front of the votive candles on the altar. Placing some change from his pocket into the slot, he lit a candle for his mother and then two more. He prayed until he felt Kara's arm around his shoulders. Then, together they walked silently from the church.

Monday, December 25

20

A Voice, A Chime, A Chant Sublime

At six o'clock on Christmas Day, the chimes in the Kingston Congregational Church tower rang out calling friends and relatives to celebrate Ruth Eddleman and Rick Carnavale's wedding.

Red and white poinsettias covered the area below the pulpit. Pine garlands with sprigs of holly and juniper berries draped the balcony railings. Tiny twinkle lights framed the windows. Arrangements of scarlet roses, ferns and baby's breath tied with silver bows hung from the end of each pew. Arthur and Samuel ushered guests to their seats and music from the organ accompanied Clay's singing in the choir loft.

Kara and Stewart began the procession followed by Sophia and Gino. Everyone smiled and waved as Rick and Ruth walked hand-in-hand down the aisle.

Before the couple spoke their vows, Arthur went forward to speak of his long friendship with Ruth and his newfound friendship with Rick.

"Ruth is loving and wise. Two of the qualities which make everyone cherish her. One of her favorite pieces of literature speaks to her wisdom. It is the scene in Thornton Wilder's Our Town when Emily says, 'Does anyone ever realize life while they live it ... every, every minute?' The Stage Manager replies, 'No. Saints and poets maybe ... they do some.' I'm sure Rick realizes that he has found both a saint and a poet in the woman who is now his life parter. And Ruth realizes what a soul mate she has found in Rick. And so I want to read to them a poem I've written in honor of their wedding day. In honor of the life they'll spend together." He unfolded a sheet of paper.

"Saints and poets clearly see
the value in the day
in hours and in minutes
time ebbing fast away
to this and that and nothing much
yet, everything, in truth
as old we grow and come to know
the transience of youth

As old we grow together in
the mist of day to day
life's happenings enfolding us
while planning all what may
But sometimes whatmay catches us
snatching time it seems
while what is present here and now
becomes just empty dreams

I'll hold your hand and promise
that I'll cherish every day
we have to hold each other close
we have to plan what may
and as we plan and life enfolds
I promise never to
be nescient of the precious time
in moments shared with you"

Ruth held the blue handkerchief belonging to Arthur's mother in her left hand. She and Rick clasped their right hands together facing each other. Friends and family listened attentively as the couple said their vows. When the minister declared the couple husband and wife, everyone burst into applause.

After the ceremony, the bride and groom stood at the entrance of the church's Fellowship Hall as people came in to greet them and their families. A table in the middle of the room was filled with platters of food and Gino ran around filling everyone's champagne glasses. He poured Kara a glass of fruit punch, "Sorry, no liquor for you. Sophia's orders."

"At least it's not green," she said to Carl and Jess Sullivan.

Clay and members of the chorus gathered round the grand piano singing Christmas songs. Buddy waltzed with Loralei while his aunt and Arthur glided around the floor to "It Came Upon a Midnight Clear". Sam, in his tuxedo and Vida, in her purple Ugly Christmas sweater made an odd couple as they did a spritely jitterbug to "Rockin' Around the Christmas Tree". Gino managed to coax some of the guests into joining him in his Peanuts Gang Dance.

"I'm surprised he's not in his Santa Claus outfit," Kara commented as people began to crowd around him hopping up and down with heads bobbing.

"I returned the costume to Clay, yesterday. And I've decided not to give Gino the Santa suit I bought him until January 6th just before we take down the decorations," Sophia informed her.

Rick patted his sister-in-law on the back. "Wise decision."

"He'll probably wear it to the baby's Christening," Ruth warned.

"He was telling me how great it would have been if you were having twin boys and you arranged for them to be born on his and Rick's birthday," Sophia informed Kara and Stewart who just stared at her in mocked horror. "Gino's really looking forward to being an uncle," she explained quickly.

"We're all looking forward to the spring," Ruth said just as Rick took her in his arms to dance to "Silver Bells".

Kara glanced around her at all of the people enjoying the celebration. "We're so lucky to be bringing a child into a place where people care so much about each other."

"I agree. The world is a tough place when you're not surrounded by people who love you." Stewart put his arms around her and they began to dance.

Just before the church bells chimed midnight, the guests escorted the bride and groom outside where a horse-drawn coach awaited them. As they rode away from the church, a song rang out from the bell tower.

"Oh, listen to that!" Ruth exclaimed. "How did they know this was my favorite Christmas carol?"

"Sophia knows everything," her husband said. "Besides, Kara remembered that you told your students how much you loved the poem when she was in your American Lit class back in college."

"I used to teach it every December. It's a poem by Henry Wadsworth Longfellow. He wrote it in 1863 during the Civil War. Even during that terrible time in our history, there was so much hope expressed in the final verses. Something we could use in any decade."

Rick moved closer, putting his arm around her and she rested her head on his shoulder. "The last carol of the season," she whispered in his ear reciting the final stanza as the bells chimed into the cold winter night.

'Til ringing, singing on its way
The world revolved from night to day
A voice, a chime,
A chant sublime
Of peace on earth, good- will to men

RESOURCES FOR CHAPTER TITLE LYRICS

1. Do You See What I See?
   from "Do You Hear What I Hear?"
   Noel Regney / music Gloria Shayne Baker 1962

2. Making a List, Checking It Twice
   from "Santa Claus Is Coming to Town"
   John Frederck Coots / music Haven Gillespie 1934

3. How Lovely Are Your Branches
   from "O Tannenbaum"
   E. Anschutz based on 16th century folk song
   by Melchior Franck / music Joachim August
   Zarnack 1824

4. Our Finest Gifts We Bring
   from "The Little Drummer Boy"
   Karen K. Davis 1957

5. You Have Termites in Your Smile, Mr. Grinch
   from "You're A Mean One, Mr. Grinch"
   Theodor S. Geisel / music Albert Hague 1966

6. Here We Come A-Wassailing
   from "Here We Come A-Wassailing"
   English Traditional c. 1850

7. Brightly Shone the Moon That Night, Though the
   Frost Was Cruel from "Good King Wenceslas"
   by John Mason Neale / music Thomas Helmore
   1853

8. Blue, Blue, Blue Holiday
   from "Blue Holiday"
   Willie Denson / Luther Dixon 1962

9. Dressed In Holiday Style
   from "Silver Bells"
   Ray Evan / Jay Livingston 1950

10. Sleep In Heavenly Peace
    from "Silent Night"
    Joseph Mohr 1816 / music
    Franz Xaver Gruber 1818

11. Fa la la la la, la la la ... laaaaaaaaah!
    from "Deck the Halls" Thomas Oliphant 1862

12. Where Are You Christmas?
    from "Christmas, Why Can't I Find You?"
    James Horner, Mariah Carey & Will Jennings 2000

13. All I Want for Christmas Is My Two Front Teeth
    from "All I Want for Christmas Is My Two Front
    Teeth" Donald Yetter Gardner 1944

14. Baby, It's Cold Outside
    from "Baby, It's Cold Outside"
    Frank Loesser 1944

15. Mary, Did You Know?
    from "Mary, Did You Know?"
    Mark Lowry / music Buddy Greene 1984

16. Oh, Tidings of Comfort And Joy
    from "God Rest Ye Merry Gentlemen"
    English Traditional 1760

17. Yeah, It Would Have Been Different Back Then
    If There Were Three Wise Women Not Three
    Wise Men from "Three Wise Women"
    Donna Opfer, Gigi Swanson &
    Anita Ridriguez 2009

18. If Only In My Dreams
    from "I'll Be Home For Christmas"
    Kim Gannon & Buck Ram /
    music Walter Kent 1943

19. Long Lay the World in Sin and Error Pining
    from "O Holy Night"
    Placide Capeau 1843 / music by Adolphe
    Adam 1847

20. A Voice, A Chime, A Chant Sublime, Of Peace on
    Earth, Good Will to Men
    from "I Heard the Bells on Christmas Day"
    Henry Wadsworth Longfellow 1863 / music by John
    Baptiste Calkin 1872

THOUGHTS ABOUT WAKEFIELD

South Kingstown is comprised of numerous little villages. One of those villages, Wakefield, became the commercial center for the town in 1907. At that time, the Narragansett Pier Railroad laid tracks along the old horse car line, up the center of town, and on out to the Narragansett seacoast resorts.

Wakefield has maintained much of its 19th century charm to this day with some of the original stores still surviving from the 1800s. Small businesses line each side of the Old Post Road, now called Main Street. Sheldon's Furniture (1857), where Detective Sullivan's parents bought their living room set, is locally renown for the structure's three-week transport down Main Street by man and oxen. It was common for buildings to be moved rather than torn down back then when Sheldon's found its new home beside the Block Building (1899), once a livery and boarding house. Dove and Distaff still provides, among other things, household goods for the discerning buyer. The Wakefield Branch (1866), where Kara's dad worked, is now Arnold's Lumber. Back in the 1890's, according to Oliver Stedman, it was "… a sociable place where groups of men liked to gather and discuss the affairs of the day …" smoking cigars from the boxes left out in the front of the store. As a boy, he vividly recalls baskets filled with eggs left on the counter and was told the local farmers used them as credit for grain or other necessities.

Kenyon's Department Store (1868) now houses other businesses. But in my mind, and in this book, Kenyon's will always remain what it was when my mom and I shopped there every Saturday four decades ago.

When I was twenty-five, I bought a house in Wakefield up on a hill on a small, dead-end street behind the town hall. The cottage was situated next door to the parish hall of St. Francis of Assisi, the oldest Catholic Church in South Kingstown. It's where Evie, Buddy, and his Aunt Suzy lit the Candle of Hope on the first Sunday in Advent. The old rectory is still next door but this stone structure, in the style of Italian Renaissance architecture, replaced the original

1870's church and was built in 1932. The Wakefield Baptist and the Episcopal Church of the Ascension on Main Street preceded the Catholic Church by a few decades.

Back in the 1970s, my mom and dad would drive from their home in Pawtucket to spend weekends with me. They loved sleeping on the lumpy, convertible couch bed on the enclosed back porch, which served as my guest bedroom. On Friday nights we'd have dinner at the nearby Larchwood Inn and on Saturday mornings, sometimes we'd have breakfast at Phil's or the local bowling alley, Old Mountain Lanes.

My dad enjoyed doing odd jobs around the house while my mother and I would head to Kenyon's, well known for the use of its large front window for creative advertising such as:

Topless Bathing Suits Sold Here
(Underneath in smaller print)
In the Men's Department

My mom especially loved the bargain basement, which reminded her of the department stores she'd worked in as a young girl. And upstairs, we tried on outfits in the ladies' dressing room, the scene of the crime in this third book of the South County Mystery Series.

Kenyon's Department Store, The Wakefield Branch, Damon's Hardware and The Larchwood Inn are no longer in business but Sheldon's Furniture, the Dove and Distaff, Old Mountain Lanes, and all three churches have survived through the intervening years. The South County Hospital has had many additions and continues to serve the community, although the pediatric ward where Sophia works no longer exists. Time marches on.

On Thursday nights this summer, along with other local vendors, Charley and I set up a table in front of Phil's, across from Brickley's Ice Cream during the weekly Riverfire events taking place along the Saugatucket River. We spent those evenings chatting with people strolling the sidewalks and selling our local mystery books. This December, the shopkeepers along Main Street will have their Annual Winter

Wonderland Celebration and, of course, the Christmas tree outside the Contemporary Theater will be lit to signal the official beginning of the Holiday Season for the village.

My parents would have loved this book. The nostalgia evoked as I wrote each scene made me stop and remember how happy we were then. I'm pleased to share some of these memories with my readers and hope you enjoy the people and places in my little part of the world.

SOURCES FROM THE SOUTH COUNTY
HISTORY CENTER

Bossy, Kathleen and Mary Keane et al. *Lost South Kingstown With a History of Ten of Its Early Villages. Wakefield* pp. 25-34. The Pettaquamscutt Historical Society, Kingston, RI, 2004.

Cotter, Betty J. *Images of America – Wakefield.* Arcadia Publishing, 1997.

State of Rhode Island and Providence Plantations Preliminary Survey Report Town of South Kingstown, Rhode Island. Historical Preservation Commission. Historic and Architectural Resources of South Kingstown, Rhode Island: A Preliminary Report, 1984

Stedman, Oliver H. *A Stroll Through Memory Lane,* Volumes I-V. Kingston Press, Inc., 1978.

Postcards from the Past

History abounds here in South County and many of the locals recorded their own memories of Wakefield in messages sent to each other on one cent postcards.

Many thanks to Mrs. Mitzi Gates for providing the following postcards of some of the places etched in my memory and used as settings in the third book in this South County Series, *Last Carol of the Season*.

Saint Francis Catholic Church on High Street in Wakefield

Larchwood Inn & Restaurant in Winter

Saugatucket River Mill Dam on Main Street in Wakefield

Wakefield Baptist Church and Rectory on Main Street in Wakefield

The Bridge Over the Saugatucket River to the Wakefield Elementary School

South County Hospital Circa 1930

ACKNOWLEDGMENTS

I've learned by the third book in the South Kingstown Mystery Series, that it takes much advice and expertise from other people to get it right. Please know these books could not have been published without the help of many people who continue to encourage and support me.

Zachary Perry, cover and interior designer and artistic young entrepreneur; Joyce L. Stevos Ph.D., who has spent countless hours editing every line and then going over the text again when I suddenly decide to make changes; beta reader, Tracy Heffron who enjoys the intricacies involved in creating mysteries as much as I do; Michael Grossman, patient formatter and publisher; Charley Sweeney, business manager, accountant, book hawker, and husband extraordinaire.

Staff of the South Kingstown History Center, Murray Gates, and Mrs. Mitzi Gates who provided historic background and postcards to enhance the pages of this book.

I'm grateful to all of you for the hours spent working with me to produce and promote my work.

To the growing number of followers of Detective Kara Langley and the South County Mysteries, thank you for your enthusiasm and your continued support and encouragement.

About the Author and Her Books

Claremary Sweeney is a writer/photographer who uses her vivid imagination to create both children's stories and adult books.

On the pages of the South County Series, Sweeney unfolds the intricate plots of her modern murder mysteries and sets them in the local historical places she knows so well – places that she holds close to her heart.

Many of the events in *Last Train to Kingston* occur in the village of Kingston not far from her home, while *Last Rose on the Vine* is set at her alma mater, the University of Rhode Island. This third book of the series, *Last Carol of the Season*, begins on Main Street in Wakefield.

Last Sermon for a Sinner is set in the village of Peace Dale. A priest has gone missing. Kara must revisit a past investigation into the disappearance of a child, to see if there are connections to the present case. This fourth book of the series will be available in the fall of 2019.

Within *A Berkshire Tale* are the original ten ZuZu stories about the adventures of a kitten born in a barn at Tanglewood who enjoys adventures at the many historic/cultural centers in western Massachusetts. Sweeney continues to write other tales in this series and is currently working on a Christmas book set in Stockbridge during the

Annual Norman Rockwell Weekend held on the first weekend of each December. Her stories appeal to the young and the young at heart.

The author lives in South County with her husband Charley and their two cats ZuZu and Roxie. Roxie hopes, some day, to have a book of her own, but for now spends time complaining about being "Roxie Dammit, aka The Other Cat" in featured posts on Ms. Sweeney's blog: Around ZuZu's Barn, Conversations With Kindred Spirits at www.aroundzuzusbarn.com